THE POISONERS

Original: *Die Giftmörderinnen* by Elfriede Czurda,
Rowohlt, Reinbek bei Hamburg 1991 ISBN 3 498 00893 5

Translated by Kathleen Thorpe

The Poisoners

Published by African Sun Media under the SUNLiT imprint

Original: *Die Giftmörderinnen* by Elfriede Czurda, Rowohlt, Reinbek bei Hamburg 1991, ISBN 3 498 00893 5

The translator and the publisher have made every effort to obtain permission for and acknowledge the use of copyrighted material. Refer all enquiries to the publisher.

Views reflected in this publication are not necessarily those of the publisher.

First edition 2020

ISBN 978-1-928314-69-1
ISBN 978-1-928314-70-7 (e-book)
https://doi.org/10.18820/9781928314707

Set in EB Garamond 11.5/14.5

Cover design, typesetting and production by African Sun Media
Cover artwork by Linda Rademan

SUNLiT is an imprint of African Sun Media. Literature and poetry are published under this imprint in print and electronic formats.

This publication can be ordered from:
orders@africansunmedia.co.za
africansunmedia.store.it.si (e-books)
Amazon Kindle: amzn.to/2ktL.pkL
Google Books: bit.ly/2k1Uilm
Takealot: bit.ly/2monsfl

Visit africansunmedia.co.za for more information.

CONTENTS

Chapter Three

TRANSLATOR'S NOTE

The Poisoners by the Austrian author Elfriede Czurda is a novel that is as fresh and relevant as when it first appeared in German in 1991. Although the crime of poisoning at first glance seems to be the pivotal point of the plot, this is deceptive. This is first and foremost a work about language, the words used to deceive and oppress women in patriarchal society where the man is ultimately the all-powerful "Word". These words are not necessarily new or even unusual in appearance but they are strung together to create a seemingly naturalised, all-encompassing web of entrapment and subjugation which Elfriede Czurda sets out to expose and dismantle. The surface fabric of false connections is meticulously unpicked to reveal the underlying structure of toxic masculinity underpinning patriarchal patterns of thought and actions which women, too are deceived into buying in to thus deterministically permeating all spheres of life in society. Translating this novel has been a rewarding challenge. Aiding the intention of disrupting the seemingly innocuous connections in language is the reversal of the tendency in German to create composite nouns, thus enabling the connecting of the previously unconnected to create new connections and meanings. Rendering this grammatical feature in English is not always linguistically possible and compromises have had to be made which, I hope, nevertheless permit a glimpse into the original authorial intention.

The contemporary relevance and topicality of *The Poisoners* belies the fact that that the novel was inspired by a murder trial that took place almost a century ago, thus perhaps also underscoring the deeply entrenched nature of patriarchy. The case was heard at the Berlin Assize Court in 1922 and the trial lasted almost a year, ending in 1923 which was significantly co-incidentally also the year of the "Beer Hall Putsch" which failed but drew attention to Adolf Hitler and the rise of National Socialism – an ideology underpinned by and actively promoting fascist-like toxic masculinity and patriarchal behaviour.

Ella Klein was accused of poisoning her husband with arsenic. Her friend, Margarete Nebbe, was accused as an accessory to the murder. On 16 March 1923 Ella Klein was convicted of the lesser charge of manslaughter and sentenced to four years in prison, while the co-accused received a jail term of just eighteen months. The outcome of the case was remarkable for the times as the progressive judge took into account that Ella had suffered abuse at the hands of her alcoholic husband, decades before the term "Battered Woman Syndrome" was coined. The case riveted the attention of Berlin society, with the added titillation of a lesbian relationship between the two women. Following the case closely was the well-known writer and medical doctor Alfred Döblin.

Döblin's interest in the case subsequently found expression in the publication of a story: Die beiden Freundinnen und ihr Giftmord (The two friends and their murder by poisoning) in 1924. His story is a blend of fact and fiction with Döblin engaging with the opinions of psychologists, psycho-sexual scientists and juristic points of view, particularly with regard to contemporary views on female criminality, as well as the difficulties in arriving at appropriate sentences. In the epilogue of his story Döblin came to the conclusion that it was impossible to fully understand the psychological factors influencing the accused. Together with these limits to understanding, Döblin also stated that he was unable to find adequate words to express the many factors motivating the crime. Döblin's story was filmed by the Austrian filmmaker Axel Corti in 1978.

In her fictional treatment of the case Elfriede Czurda takes up the challenge facing Döblin by innovatively subjecting language to scrutiny in order to gain an understanding of what could have lain in the background of the murder. By unravelling the everyday surface of the "normal" fabric if language she exposes the warp and weft of patriarchy and attendant toxic masculinity supporting the oppression of women. By structuring the plot around the interrelationship of four women, Elfriede Czurda skillfully attacks the silence surrounding abuse leading to the poisoning as a desperate way out of an intolerable situation: Else, the wife of Hans, her possessive girlfriend Erika, Erika's mother, the enabler and Mrs. Rinx, Else's grotesquely venomous mother-in-law – "patriarchy in drag" to borrow a term from Marc Lamont Hill. This is no black- and-white story – all are perpetrators and all are victims, even Hans.

Kathleen Thorpe

ABOUT THE COVER

The artwork on the cover formed a component of my solo exhibition in partial fulfilment of my M Tech FA, completed in 2017 at UJ. The dissertation was titled *Threads of ambivalence; redressing selected aspects of Afrikaner female identities through art making.* The artwork was titled *In the name of the father.*

In the name of the father
The lower case 'f' in father refers to ¡SEP¡ men and not the Lord. The Bible, a book written by men, prescribes that women should be silent and that they should defer to men, as for example in 1 Tim. 2:11-13 (Holy Bible, NIV): "A woman should learn in quietness and full submission. I do not permit a woman to teach or to assume authority over a man; she must be quiet." I have addressed this Calvinistic power relation by covering the christening dress in embroidered verses from the Scriptures, denouncing women as individuals in their own right and denying women their own voice.

The verses embroidered (subversive stitching) on the christening dress reinforce what is expected of the girl child, who is symbolically inducted into her place in society, where she is expected to honour, submit to and be subservient to men.

The incorporation of used teabags in conjunction with the act of sewing these teabags together creates an altered state that introduces a conceptual reading where the medium becomes the message. The artwork, being executed in the very medium of women's oppression, that is, needlework historically executed in the home as part of a woman's domestic duties, is suggested as a post-modern symbol of women's defiance.

The christening dress is displayed in an archival cabinet, rather than being placed in a frame. The archival cabinet is used to refer to the out-dated notion of women's silence. As this 'silence' belongs in the past, it is treated as a relic of history and preserved as such, because it is no longer relevant.

Linda Rademan

ACKNOWLEDGEMENTS

I wish to gratefully acknowledge the support of all those who have made the publication of my translation of *The Poisoners* possible. The Österreichische Gesellschaft für Literatur, Vienna, generously supported visits to Vienna. Elfriede Czurda has my sincere gratitude for her enthusiastic support of this project, generosity of spirit, sacrifice of time and patience. I learned so much from her about how meaning is negotiated. My special thanks go to Linda Rademan for graciously permitting her artwork to be used for the cover illustration and to African Sun Media for their care and attention. Thank you, too, to my friends for their support and interest.

Chapter One

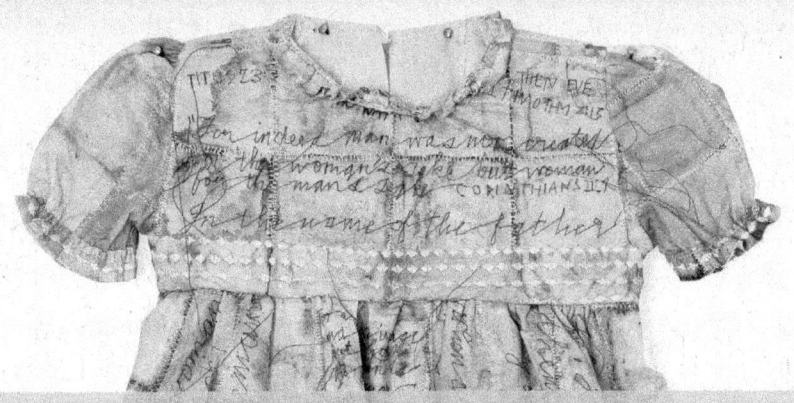

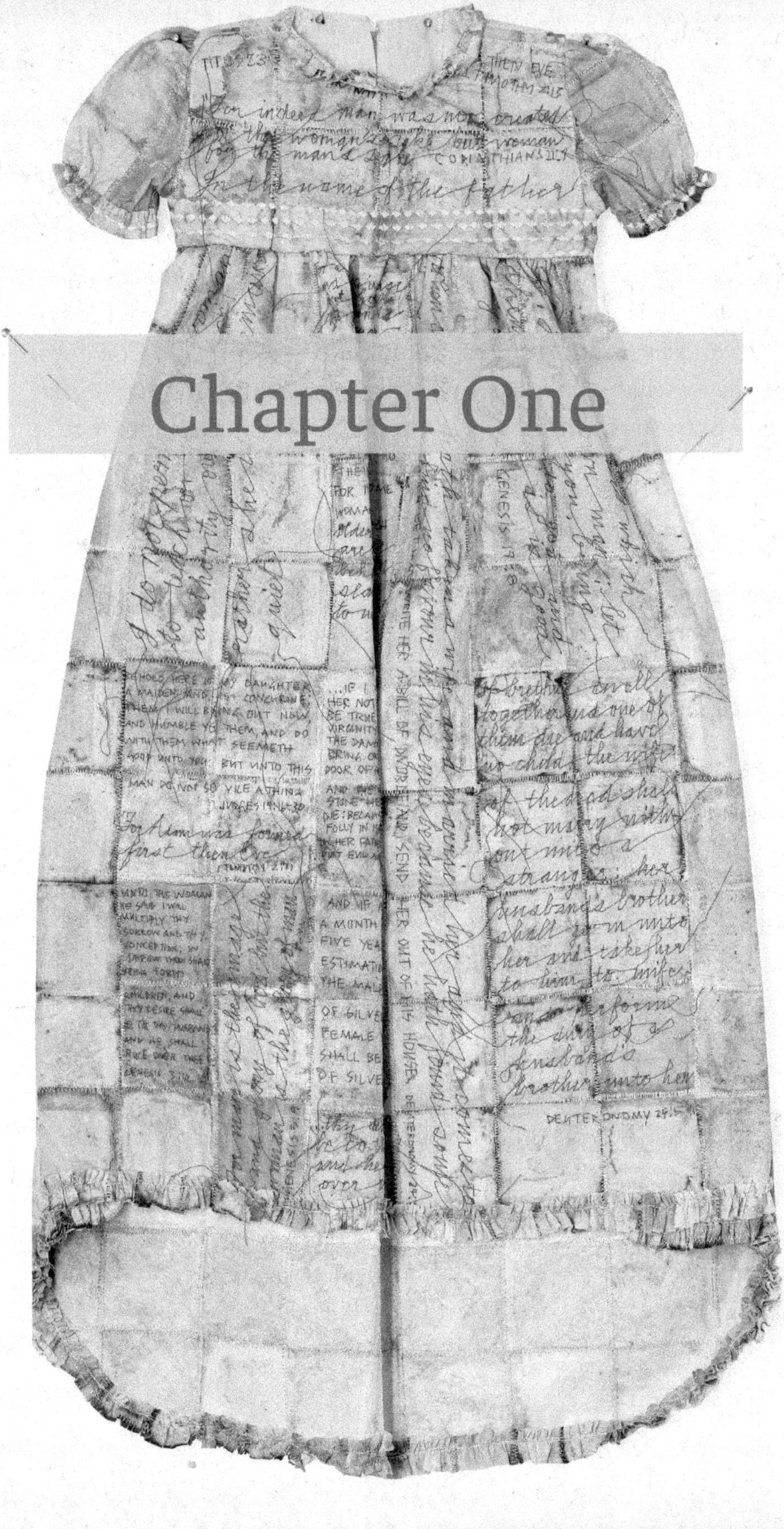

For indeed man was not created for the woman's sake but woman for the man's sake
In the name of the father
JUDGES 19:16-30
DEUTERONOMY 24:5

1.   THE CELL

The small patch cut out of the blue. In this keep coop crouches Else. She sends her gaze: outside! It entices her: follow me follow me! Ever deeper into the blue. Come come we will flash. Come we will flit we will reach its base. We will look past the Dog Star – past Sirius. Stars stars. The border of the Milky Way flickers into focus. But onward. Onward. Here the faraway moves further all the more.

Hans, shouts Else, are you there, Hans?

I am here Hans, says Else, for the next few years. Whenever you return from your travels, says Else, in case. If there is a soul, says Else, in case, and the young craftsmen are not on their way for longer than that either.

Else stares into the square, gawks into the blue. It draws back before her gaze. Continually back. Else moves out on this path. As high as they rise, as high as she propels her glances, they do not advance. *Back. Back.* Over there her lens darts. With her eye Else marks the patch *Heaven*. Patches the *Firmament* together. The *Ether*, Perfect Lover L(over), devours the dick end of her thoughts and her body that dangles from it. This actual keep within the keep. Cause of all ruin.

Hans do not serenade me otherwise the heavens will be full of you! Hans do not serenade this keep, it is a coffin a coffin.

It is not a little death.

It is the big one.

2.   THE BODY

Else has a Body. There is never any way past it. She never grows into it. Never does she put her thoughts into this hideous bag. Never again will anybody reach to lay hold of this butcher's block. Reach for this fish smell centre that is turned inside. To who knows where. Else shudders. Gulps. Never! Now they are all locked out thankgoodness. Hans. And Erika. These voices attached to a body of flowing blood.

They remain behind bars thankgoodness. Here their voices go out and in but otherwise not a filament, not a foot, not a finger. This cowardly Erika! She must not show herself. She can gnaw away at herself with pleasure. She should shiver. Betrayer! Malicious hypocrite. Perjured pig! Every single oath a lie. Every single Word a swindle. Every armpit every yard every arse (Else blushes) an artifice.

Then we'll be free.

Then we'll be independent.

Then there will be evermore only us two in the world.

Unceasingly you and me for ever and ever.

What sort of freedom then Else if not even the eye reaches far enough? What sort of freedom if the escaping gaze loses its direction. If it scatters like a sheaf and wanders around aimlessly in this blue without edges. Without a border. Without focus and fuzziness.

Who is free then? Is Erika free? Tied to her mother's apron strings. Attached to Mamma's navel. Trolling for an escape. No no. Else is free of the others because there is a wall around her. A work of construction through which no strange hand is conducted. In this destiny no unauthorised person can interfere. No coy pretense. Hans. Could be that Hans is free in his own way. Could be, if Else gazes past the nebula that is called Magellan, could be, over there is Hans. If she sees him, out there in the blue heavens, she will say HansIloveyou. Else knows exactly that then she will love him very much, this thought in heaven that is called Hans. Only the disembodied Hans loves his Else as he should. Without this private parts pillory pole paw prrrr brrrrr! Else burns from blushing. Her head will explode. So that it, unfragmented, has room in the cell. And all the thoughts in it! It is settlement-day. Execution! May Day Dance.

3. THE POLKA AND THE WORDS AND THE LETTER

Hans fetches Else for the Polka. HansTheGlance. He fixes his gaze on Else. Hard as a rock he looks at Else, in the blink of an eye he constructs his eyrie in her.

Elsechickgorgeousyou you are like a colibri that I saw in the zoo. Each feather is of a different colour, not merely like a peacock that has different colours but the same on each feather. Something that special you are to me, Elsechickgorgeousyou, each separate feather extra bright.

Hans spoke to Else like that. More beautifully than she had ever heard before. Hans speaks like a Poet but rarely. Otherwise he is worse than the animal of which he speaks. He says nothing at all about that. Not a sound.

Light as a birch Hans dances with Else. Sends out the tendrils of his hand like a leaf in the wind around Else's dress. So delicately. Not this immediate grabbing and groping. No hard wood with the Polka. The Else is a bit of fluff in this air current HansTheGlance. Else is a speck of dust that settles on the Planet Hans. The Planet Hans is heavy when he lays himself on top of Else. But the bird brain Else cannot think such connections. Where each and every Hans has his brain as a matter of course, every Else has a boggy swamp, out of which smelly blisters of feeling bubble up. The nether regions of every Else begin right beneath her hairline. For this reason Else thinks she is a pinch of down in the mild general climate of HansTheGlance. Thinks she can easily remain outside as a flock. The wreath on the maypole spreads out. The velvet blue sky extends itself up above. The magnificent stars sparkle in it. Hans doesn't flirt. What he says is a Word.

Elsechickgorgeousyou you are like a sea. That glistens. That rocks me. I see it in your eye. It rocks to and fro. I am lying on the seabed in complete tranquility. Eternal silence gazes at me, you blue sea eye. Elsechickgorgeous, your gaze is a promise unto death when I look at you.

Rapidly Hans extends his fortress. Pegs out his claim. Already he is ruling over life and death. Over taking and taming. With tooth and nail he mars his adornment. He transcribes his Else so that Else is written off from the beginning. With this copy in calligraphy Hans frames his empty interior spaces. So that it is nice inside of himself. And all around outside Hans makes attempts on the entire botched Else who is lacking something here, there and everywhere. Nobody should say anything about it. Else can be grateful that the thoroughly magnanimous HansTheGlance is taking her with all her enormous defects.

These deficiencies! There Else does not want to even begin counting. The list is endless. Just like the blue in the square cut-out. Trimmed to shape with no end either.

Elsechickgorgeousyou you are like a blank white sheet of paper on which I am the Word. You are all around me in complete purity. You are like the nothingness that I first efface because I have Words to put into the emptiness. Because I am the Word so-to-say. Within the rhythm moving me you are the interval in which I confidently take my afternoon tea. Elsechickgorgeousyou, I thirst after you.

Thus the Words go in and out of Else. Without door. Without knocking. Else does not have a bolt against the Words in her body. They live with her in the cell. Owing to them she will grow swollen in the course of time. Else is quite sure indeed. If they do not want to come out of her, Else will die of them.

Else is quite sure indeed.

The blue space behind the square is vast. A boundlessly vast valley. Else gazes into the uninhabited nothingness. Who knows if it is uninhabited. Somewhere over there are the souls, in case. Not that they live with house and table and chair. They are a thought that one sees, if. Or hears. That over there someone says *Hans*. Or that Hans is written over there. In capital letters HANS in the black-blue heavens. A Word that nobody can write any more. That is only here if one is over there at that black place. Far behind the Magellan Cloud. Always presupposing: if. How is Else supposed to know that? She is not able to, Hans always says. Else feels conscious of how right Hans is. Else feels, she is especially fearful of what she does not know. She is a fishing fly as Hans knows. She is a wash-out as Hans knows. Knew. Now Else is alone with all that. With everything that is dangerous. With everything that she fears. She is now eye-to-eye with all the dull opacities.

But at least she is immured behind thick walls. They protect her a little. Even if only from the world. Even if not from Hans. Nor from Erika.

Now Hans is gone it is true. But his Words are still stuck in Else's Body. They remain. They are hooked into this abandoned tract of land. They have branded Else. They have larded Else. Her skin is a running sore of Words. They cannot get in. Nor out. From out if this scarred crust nothing escapes. The wilderness festers and ferments. Else does not notice the puss. She does not have any such body. This paunch with arms and legs does not belong to her. She is not sensible of it. She does not know it. She does not move it. It does not follow her orders. It walks woodenly. It walks from memory. Else has no contact with it. She washes it, nothing more. Martial law is prevailing now.

Dear Elsiebabefairy are you coming at last this afternoon? I'll tell you how I would like to love you and you're continually not here and you say you're not coming and H is to blame and you're always pushing me away. Always. Because of him. As I would always like to love you with my feelings and prove it to you, too. Please place the geranium on the left! Do you hear? Don't just simply forget me Elsiebabefairy. You shouldn't do that eternally! Ek.

Else is burnt over her entire body by a foreign flesh. Stamped. Nailed. Sewn up. Like harpoons it has been shot into her. Like the arrows of a crossbow it rummages around in her. Hansthewolf. Hanshyena. As if he wanted to gouge new openings into the cloak of her skin. As if he wanted to shred this cloak and don it himself. The Sharp Tooth Jackal. Else prefers to think of *him*. She does not know him at least. He attacks her disinterestedly. He does not mean it like that. Then he goes again. Hans stays. Stayed.

Erika stays and stays. Drives her torsions further into Else's bugle. Brain. Skulks behind the door, the everlasting carbuncle. Has only one Word at her disposal. Honks, the stuck gramophone, Love. Love Love Love. Unflinchingly Love, the groove. This underdeveloped female memory has catapulted out all commonsense. It stupidly repeats the one syllable, crutch of obsession which is a torrent. Else does not know how to swim at all! Else spins from one swirl to the next. The undertow never lets her go.

Dear Elsiebabefairy there's still no answer and the geranium is still standing around and I've been waiting for more than two hours! If you don't love me anymore say so and don't play around with me and use me like a discarded toy and hurt me as it suits you. Such a Love is something great and unique and only you and I are capable of such a thing and we have to just keep silent and suffer and hope. And stick together! Eternally yours Ek.

Else shudders.

Else finds it difficult to cope with these attacks. She is lying on her back. On the slat-bed. She is sopping wet with perspiration. Soon she is no longer able to breathe. That is Purgatory. That the Words do not cease.

Up above the velvet violet sky. The colourful ribbons on the maypole wreath. The silvery night air calls. What, Else cannot make out. The maypole is as high as the sky. The Hope! The Proposal! The trumpeters chirp like cymbals. They grind the barrel organ like aeolian harps. That is the need which the proposal calls forth.

Hans grabs the Else where she is lacking. He leads her home. There he immediately hands her over to his Mamma as a gift. The Mamma is really dissatisfied. Then everything is fine. Then Hans can go to work.

4. THE DESIRES

Mrs. Rinx is the Mamma. She lives in the small room next to the kitchen. Else and Hans live in the other room. With a pair of scissors Mrs. Rinx cuts a hole in every one of Hans's shirts. Then she tips over the pot of boiling milk a bit. Predictably the milk runs over, forms skin blisters, settles into every groove on the stove plate, runs hissing through the stoke-hole right into the fire, bakes stinking on the white enamel, leaving traces of dried-up streams.

Else you slattern, shouts Mrs. Rinx so that the neighbours hear.

Else you slovenly slut your milk, screeches Mrs. Rinx and quickly tilts the pot once more.

Mrs. Rinx grins. She is able to defend herself well against her rival co-plaintiff. Mrs. Rinx demands everything. For herself. She finally wants to produce a Present Time for her desires. No, she is not going to land in a vague Future any longer. That is and remains at where Mrs. Rinx will never arrive. What kind of rosy promises have faded there during the course of her life. Always in front of her nose so that they exhaust themselves. Always behind the glass wall which she never shatters. So that she can never really reach there. What sort of essential crimes have darkened away over there. Undone. Now Mrs. Rinx is hitting back. Around herself. Until she is through to the other side, through this impenetrable Plexiglas. She spares no-one. And even if she destroys what she holds dear. What Mrs. Rinx can lose had already been lost before the start. This time Mrs. Rinx is going to win! And even if it means death. She is not going to let any desire fall away any more. No-one with ears to hear had ever heard rattling on the floor of reality. What there really is, says the late departed Mr. Rinx, makes a noise. What he does not hear, says the late departed Mr. Rinx, does not exist. So it is with the desires, the late departed Mr. Rinx explains. Mrs. Rinx wishes everything for herself. Her memory flashes. Out from the abyss of failures all warning lights are flashing. No, thunders the late departed Mr. Rinx. He has his reasons. Mrs. Rinx wishes for herself especially: Happiness! A pressure cooker! A pair of black court shoes for festive occasions. Health! A garden with dahlias, asters, gladioli, daisies, carrots, kohlrabi, radishes and the whole nine yards. A diamond ring with a large stone even if it does not show up well on her work-roughened hands. The Pensions Clerk Kümmler should have a stroke the rotten nut! A glass shade for the bedside table lamp. A white Angora cat Kitty who always purrs whenever she sees Mrs. Rinx. World Peace. A nice pensioner who strokes her breasts. Who lugs the heavy bags up to the second floor like the late departed Mr. Rinx. He should not be too decrepit. Lace curtains for the kitchen window where in a row nothing but little white houses and little white swans and little white poplar trees are woven into the lace. In general a Golden Ass! Mrs.Rinx winks.

Her real desires remain in a sanctuary. Mrs. Rinx does not enter them in any list. No human being will become aware of them. She will take these with her to the grave. She always immediately had an abortion. No law is able to prohibit that. Hans is the vault of her desires. Before him Hans's father was the family grave for the female Rinx's desire, before that the Papa of Mrs. Rinx née Rappel. A good family praises tradition. Her Hans Rinx deserves something better. That stands in every book. If he honoured his Mother he would not bring such a worthless stray Else home to her. Oh yes, they're running around in their hundreds. What is Mrs. Rinx saying they're running around here, there and everywhere in their thousands! But her good son is such a good Hans. Shows his first-rate Mamma just what kind of an outstanding Mrs. Rinx she is. And remains a warrior heroine, the Mrs. Rinx. In this entire clawed female brood she is the sable. So she gilds her golden sceptre Hans. He is her success. She would most of all like to devour him. And reproduce him again. He should turn out so well again, her happy event. He sprouted out of just the right place. Stupid that he's a male member that dropped off from the Mamma. Into the lap of every stray Else. That has to stop! Immediately!!!

Else yells Mrs. Rinx piercingly, stinking stable scour the warts of milk off the stove! Or what is supposed to become of that you barren blank?

Else closes the bedroom door. She takes the milk pot off the stove. She puts it in the sink. She takes her knitted cardigan from the chair. She shuts the flat door.

Now Else only returns when Hans is there long since returned from work. Mrs. Rinx can rule alone over floorboards, curtains, kitchen cupboards and foodstuffs. Nothing happens that is not commanded by Mrs. Rinx. Mrs. Rinx does not order anything. Hans will see, she does not interfere. Hans will see her reticence. There is no meal on the table. No washing up has been done. No shirt has been mended. No laundry has been ironed. Mrs. Rinx does not interfere with destiny. She does not make life difficult for any Else. She withdraws to her retirement plot. To her position of rest. From over there she means well. She on her own would be able to make things so nice for Hans. But then a stray Else had to come into the house. Had to bring confusion into the kitchen. Had to cause a man so much sweat on his brow. Has to rob a mother of her son. Mrs. Rinx is a thoroughly organised Mrs. *Hans* Rinx. The Else fades there into complete invisibility. One sees a Mrs. Rinx so much better, the less Else shows herself. An Else is and remains a train smash. Takes to her heels. Always poised for flight, always nailed to the spot, she will not escape. Lives in dumb silence. The mouth says no Word. The hand says no Word. The face says no Word. What is under her clothing says even less. What the Else says comes out of Hans's mouth. Hans reads what dwells beneath the clothes. He does not tell tales to his Mamma.

Where is Else, asks Hans, who comes home.

Don't ask me, says Mrs. Rinx. She doesn't tell me anything after all. Ask Else where she is. She knows where she'd rather stay. She knows why. Don't ask me.

When did Else go out, asks Hans who has just come home.

Don't ask me, says Mrs. Rinx. She goes out when I'm in my room. Ask Else when she goes away. Ask Else where she drifts around for so long. You may not ask me.

Why did Else go out, asks Hans who has just come in through the door from work.

Just don't ask me, says Mrs. Rinx. Else is a good-for-nothing. Else is not a Good Wife. Otherwise she wouldn't have gone away without cooking for you. She would have stayed here and would have washed the dishes. She would have mended these shirts here. She would have spun a little thread. She would have sent a little song to greet her husband. For sure she'll put the blame on Mrs. Rinx.

Hans sits down at the table. He is silent. He doesn't eat anything. No, Mrs. Rinx doesn't need to make him anything. No, he's not hungry. Hans keeps silence and stares fixedly at the geranium. For a long time Hans stares at the geranium by the window. Mrs. Rinx doesn't know what Hans sees over there. Mrs. Rinx does not know what is to be thought about the geranium. To think for so long and to brood. She could make things so nice for him on her own, the Mrs. Rinx. But Hans doesn't listen. There are only Hans and the geranium in the whole flat. Everything else is air. Mrs. Rinx is air, too. Hans gets up. He puts on his jacket. He shuts the flat door.

Mrs. Rinx does not understand that. There goes her own flesh and blood. What Mrs. Rinx desires goes out by the door. Inconsiderately shuts the flat door. Leaves the yawning abyss and the night to Mrs. Rinx. Mrs. Rinx is alone with the geranium, about which she can now ruminate. Mrs. Rinx goes to the window. She pushes the geranium aside. She airs the room. Outside the twilight is approaching. It sparkles glassily. It ignites everything that can sparkle.

5.   THE BETRAYAL

You betrayed it, groans Erika and clutches herself at forehead and heart! You've betrayed everything!

No, says Else. She plucks at the sleeve of her pink knitted cardigan. Definitely not, says Else and bows her head.

She's lying! howls Erika. She's lying, she's lying she's lying! Then she howls wordlessly.

No, says Else.

What's going on, says Mrs. Runk, Erika's Mamma. What's going on what's going on. Just keep cool. Mrs. Runk strokes the squeaking head of her Erika.

She wouldn't be a liar, says Mrs. Runk. She needs you.

No, cries Erika shrilly, of course!

Else plucks at the sleeve of her woolen cardigan. Inside her head she gazes over there across the road at what no Erika sees. She does not need to lift her head. It is the house made of lead. It is on the other side of the street. It is the number fifteen. No other house in the world is as dark. No other house is so heavy that one balks. None other takes one's breath away in such a way whenever one has to enter there. None other suffocates one in such a way. None other overwhelms one in such a way up and down the lane. No other house in the city is like this.

Else hears Erika sniff and blow her nose. In her bowed head Else sees Erika sniffing and blowing her nose.

A window is open in the lead-grey house. A crack. How well Else knows the window! It is the window of Else's cage. It is Else's geranium that is standing at the window. It is standing very far to the left at the window. It is meagre. Its dwindled stem is emaciated. The pink blossom is haggard. A starving little tree forms its bowed image in Else's eye. *I love you but have to stay here*, says the plant which only Erika interprets. And Else. Else had not brought it to speech. Else had not tweaked it. Now the geranium cannot keep quiet anymore. It is always prattling something.

Lie betrayal betrayal! shrieks Erika and claws herself into Mamma's skirt.

Else sits stiffly at the table. She sits speechlessly on the edge of the chair. She has been petrified forever, it seems to Else. She cannot stand up anymore. She cannot walk anymore. No arm can lift her up. She cannot move a leg. She is a piece of granite that is very heavy and very hard. She is the most rigid rock that a piece of granite can be. As this rock that she is, Else is capable of pulverizing the world. As this rock that she is, she is capable of causing an annihilation. Nobody will escape. Nobody will remain. There will be nobody who will be able to recover from this. There will be nobody who will ever laugh about the rock who is Else. But she cannot budge from the spot. She is like rock. Where it struck her. No higher motivation sets her rolling. Inside is the secret that she has preserved. That is now a rock, too.

I have to go, says Else and stands up. Else is surprised. I am going, says the surprised Else. And wants to leave by the door.

No, cries Erika, not! Erika darts between Else and the door.

Now I am going, says Else and takes a step.

Please Else stay a while, whimpers Erika, Mamma is bringing a glass of eggnog.

The Mamma quickly brings Else a glass of eggnog.

Else drink, pleads Erika, drink and swear that you'll never. That you'll never ever, Else. Under no circumstances.

It is already completely dark, says Else.

Else goes.

She'll come again my child, says Mrs. Runk. She has to go and is coming again, assures Mrs. Runk, it's dark.

Just like Karl, rages Erika, just like Karl Mamma?

But Erika.

Is it always dark? Because Karl never comes.

But child but child.

Mamma help me, yowls Erika.

It's alright it's alright, soothes Mrs. Runk Aren't we together my child? Isn't your Mamma with you forever?

But *Karl*, Mamma!

Karl made a Married Woman out of you, maintains Mrs. Runk. That is decent. That's more than one can expect, explains Mrs. Runk.

I want to have Karl here! I want to have Else here! storms Erika. To have here have here have here! Erika rages over and away past Mrs. Runk.

As long as you have a Mother, consoles Mrs. Runk.

The Mamma switches off the light. Now it's dark in the flat. Soon it will become peaceful in the inhabitants. They are sleeping.

6.   THE BED AND THE MOTHER

From out of every pore Else forces a drop of sweat. It is a Word that is driven out from every pore. The twilight paints the window bars with black lines. The background of the sky is made of molten ash. Here time must please make a stop. If a lead pencil sketches the sky with bars in front of it, it can likewise draw Else with a few strokes behind her, too. If Else is flat, with two dimensions, no sweat can come out of her. If no sweat comes out of Else, there cannot be any more Words in Else either. The torment will be at an end. But it is a sharpened pencil without mercy. At the window it makes a stop with the flat surface and the two elongations.

It leaves Else space that she does not like at all. It does not annihilate the Word torpedoes that scrape around in Else. Which hammer in the slag-heaps of the unspeakable.

When Else comes home it is completely dark. It is very quiet when Else arrives home. It is dismally dark and silent at Else's home. Else soundlessly unlocks the door. In the dark she softly closes the door. She hurriedly slips to the kitchen table. Inaudibly she pulls back the chair. Soundlessly she sits down. Silently Else lays her head on her arms. In her head is now dead silence. Hopefully.

Hopefully Hans Rinx is already at home. Hopefully Hans Rinx is already sleeping in the bedroom. Hopefully Else will soon hear her Wedded Husband Hans Rinx snoring. It is so quiet in the flat.

It is so dreadfully quiet in the Rinx rooms.

It reverberates with silence and seclusion in the House of Rinx.

Breathlessly Else dozes off. Hastily Else wants to slumber a bit. Else wants to tarry a while in the head graveyard. Over there a fly buzzes. Buzzes and buzzes around Else's heavy empty head.

The darkness outside is so similar to the gloom inside. The one conceals itself in the mimicry of the other. Else could almost take one for the other, the blackness in the cell and the black painting in front of the image cut-out. With her hand before her eyes, Else cannot see. But the white of the eye ball glimmers in the mirror above the wash basin. The mirror places a second cut-out universe into the close cage. Two worlds greasy with clouds. Two gullets black with fear. Does Else live in both of them? Are all the piercing pricking Words in her duplicated in the end? The Word harpoons of Hans. Mirrored in the stickling syllable stabbing grappling irons of Erika? Like an echo all around in Else hurled, broken, amplified? The walls of the cell are serrated with chatter order screaming swigging clamour. They will close in around Else like an Iron Maiden.

Else starts up into alertness.

The door-handle moves. The door- handle of Mrs. Rinx moans very softly in two angles. Almost inaudibly the door swings open. In creeps Mrs. Rinx on the tips of her toes and yaps. Mygoodnessyoumonster, you most likely want to scare me to death! Mrs. Rinx walks clumsily in sheep's wool socks over to the refrigerator. You want to nibble titbits on the sly for sure.

Mygoodnessyoumonster, what are you doing lolling about here at the table! Mrs. Rinx cancels a night's rest. Are you a fish? Or are you my Hans's pillow of repose? The condition for my continued existence? Intobedwithyoutoyourhusband!

Mrs. Rinx clatters in the crockery cupboard so that her son hears it. Mrs. Rinx clatters with the milk bottles in the refrigerator so that her son knows the situation and deals with his property. Mamma Rinx announces vigilance. Mamma Rinx demands self-effacing sacrifice. A lifelong fortune is lying on the plate.

What sort of a din is this then, grumbles Hans from out of the bedroom door.

What sort of an uproar and clattering is this in the middle of the night, the red Hans face scolds into the kitchen.

What sort of a rumbling and outcry and shouting without end is here when one wants to sleep in the night, thunders the countenance of Hans ready to strike in a torrent of an irritability. A well-known fire fans out from Hans into the kitchen. An instilled fright frenzy unfurls its flag out of Hans. Out of the booze bog Hans Rinx. An inordinate desire casts its noose. Up from the sediment of the swamp a fettering lash lifts lasciviously. Slat-bed. Slot. Hans does not know precisely.

Offintobedwithyouyoustrayinghussy. Youmangybitchintothepen.

Hans drags Else into bed. Here there is nothing Else can do. Only Hans does something. Hans says nothing. He tosses around in the bed and does not sleep. Else is not able to change that. Hans thrashes the sheet and holds onto Else. Else holds her Breath. Else lashes her Lungs tightly. Else bites her Lips sore. Else moans with her Mouth. Else groans loudly and cannot stop anything. Her Body does not speak. It keeps silence. It is laid waste. It mocks the sounds Else makes. It dams up rigidly around the bones, far removed from every Else. How dark it is.

How terribly ominous is the march through the night without stopping. And does not come to an end. Most of all Else wants to scream Help. Else does not want to call out more than that. Only Help. Else would gladly suffocate. Death-rattle. Become paralyzed in the stench from the yawning mouth. Else wants to break her neck. Slip. Collapse in the sour sweat. And willingly perish.

There! There is a Hand. Seeking the Thighs. Will presently find them. Has five frightful Fingers for raking about. Has Fingers that burrow. Like mole holes. Like worms. Draw out a thread of slime. Contaminate the whole area with mucilage. The mattress groans and creaks. Hans breathes heavily.

Hans pants. Hans sweats. What comes now, thank God, happens in a Past that Else no longer remembers. Thank God. Else wakes up in a Future where what is coming now is over.

Hans hurls himself onto Else. Rolls himself onto her. Stretches himself out under her. Lifts a leg up high straightens his back turns his neck revolves his hips opens his mug and drips off sweat spreads his toes wide licks the Ears gnaws the Nose clutches the Hips. Pants. Groans. Shrieks. Spits. Grunts. Squeals. Babbles. Pokes into Else straightens his rump. Listens intently. Stiffens.

Remains rigid in Else that is some kind of command.

The door is opened. The light is switched on. The radio is turned on. Mamma Rinx is standing in the room. She is naked. She dances a waltz. Her hip joints grate. She heavily heaves her leg high. She swivels her pelvis. Her belly folds flick. She points her toes. She bends her knees. She extends her breasts. Fondles them with her fingers. She twists her nipples. Drink, Hans dearest Son. She wrenches her wrist. She strokes her thigh. She grips her groin. She curls her pubic hair. Hans, she pants from deep inside her entrails, Hans, dearest son.

Hans groans. Hans gasps. Hans penetrates with the stream into the biology. Hansshameonpippi, moans Hans. He throws himself down on the nuptial bed. He thrusts into the bedside cabinet door. He takes out his napkins.

He reaches into the bedside cabinet drawer. Hans fetches his dummy. He gropes in the bedside cabinet. Hans brings his toweling nappy and lays it before Else. Else whimpers. Else grizzles and sobs and howls.

Hans you whore, shouts Mamma Rinx. Resounding shrilly Mamma Rinx stumbles from the room.

Switchoffthelightelse.

Switchoffthelightelse. There is no light. Never. Else's eyes are internal spotlights. Even if Else closes her eyes, it never becomes dark. Even with closed eyes Else stares into a brightly-lit panoptikon. A glisteningly distinct Mrs. Rinx roams through every darkest night. An aging naked Rinx Mother Body lies in wait in every darkest prison. In every blackest dungeon a babbling Hans kicks about in napkins. Sucks on Mamma's nipples. That is the Inferno in Else's memory. That is a creeping-barrage in her head that incinerates all thoughts. That is until death a burning bomb-shell legacy. Is able to ignite until way after the End of the World.

Help, screams Else. Else cannot stand it. It drives her insane.

It tears her apart. Else implores. Blindly Else takes to the wind.

Else lies unconscious in the cell.

Keep cool good child, says the good Father, you are with me where it is good.

A good Woman, says the good Father, speaks only really good things of her Wedded Husband in the good Future.

Without a Husband, says the good Father, my good Else is not real.

What you always all know thank God good Father.

It is all good good Father thank God even death.

7. THE CHAIN SWINGER AND THE NIGHT MARE

Come! calls Erika. Else come! Let's ride once more on the Chain Swinger. Once more and once more again. I'll fly behind you. Right through the air. Come Else! giggles Erika. We'll simply fly. And not stop any more.

Else cuts through the singing wind. Beneath Else the tent the stalls and the houses rush past. Else reaches into the blue afternoon. Only this little bit of chain link is hooked into a mooring. Else leans forward into eternity. She tilts toward the distant blue.

Hurrah I'll catch you, Erika reaches her in her absent-mindedness. Else is startled. No do not catch me, says Else.

Nobody should catch Else. No-one should take hold of Else. Else wants to fly solo. Up up and die down. In front of Else is this hope which is a windy vacant form. An unknown gay spark elevates Else into this high future lap. The empty air ship shall reach up for the stars. It shall run along. Without anything. Simply just like that. Somehow Else will then expire in the fire. Somehow Else will then become a chaste thought. That does not need a Word. It is not moist and has no blood heat.

Else! calls Erika.

Else! calls Erika and shakes Else by the shoulders. Don't stay away for so long in your thoughts Elsiebabefairy. Your thoughts are mine, Elsiebabefairy and mine are of course uninterruptedly with you, too with warmth and understanding. Come Elsiebabefairy set your feet back into reality again, because of course you belong to me, Erika, forever and into all eternity.

Erika is always calling Else back. Back into spaces where there is pain. Back to warm moist disgusting places. Where it reeks and steams.

Else tries to defend herself and gasps. Terror shackles Else. It constricts her. Else is always entangled in thick ropes. Knotted and firmly moored with anchor-cables. Somebody or something is always in possession of Else. Gusts of rain chase past the cell window. The elements shake at the foundations. Else shakes at her concatenation. The night mare is able to come in by the door and window. It cannot find its way out anywhere. With non-degradable plastic cords it is wrapped around Else.

Mrs. Runk knocks at the Rinx family door. Politely Mrs. Runk knocks at the front door of the Rinx family.

Erika sent me, says Mrs. Runk. Erika has a mishap. Erika is languishing from a lack. Erika is suffering from a shortage. A change. Else could surely revive, Mrs. Runk inquires. Else could surely augment, reconnoiters Mrs. Runk. Do you and your son fare well? imposes Mrs. Runk. Erika is a lot in life, laments Mrs. Runk. That must unfortunately be taken into account. Her frame of mind permits an urgent request, the helpful Mrs. Runk invents. But I am entreating you, she entreats Mrs. Rinx. We Mothers, assures Mrs. Rinx. That goes without saying, We Mother Hearts, Mrs. Runk.

Else takes her knitted cardigan from the chair and accompanies Mrs. Runk. Else slips into the pink woolen waistcoat and slips out of the flat with Mrs. Runk.

Else and Mrs. Runk hasten from the Rinx house. Else leans her head against Erika's door-jamb and weeps. Else retches every drop of liquid out of her body. Else sobs soundlessly into her handkerchief. Else leans rigid and benumbed against the wooden edge and whimpers. Else trembles. Else twitches.

Is it better is it good? Asks Mrs. Runk. She caresses Else on the head.

Is it better is it good? Asks Erika. She caresses Else on the cheek.

I will be dead, says Else. And Else says: I will be dead. I will be dead I will be dead I will be dead.

Erika takes Else by the hand. Timidly Else looks at Erika. Erika seats Else at the table. Erika puts a glass of eggnog before Else. She strokes Else's hand head back. *I will be dead*, calls the geranium at Else's window. If the stem points to the north it means *I will be dead*. When the geranium speaks, Mrs. Runk will come, Erika and Else have sworn to one another. If the geranium calls *Death*, Erika will send her Mother over immediately, Erika and Else have sworn to one another. It is still standing over there, the geranium, and calling after Else *I will be dead*.

Is it good is it good now? asks Mrs. Runk. She pours liqueur.

Is it good is it good now? asks Erika. She holds out the glass to Else.

Else shakes her head. Else keeps silent and shakes her head. The tears flow from the red eyes of the silent Else.

Gasping Else finally awakes. Rain rattles onto the window. It is still pitch dark. Is it perhaps near morning? These internal prison debacles do not want to come to an end. No full stop is found by the picture plots in this long seamy sideshow. Like an endless silent movie they haunt an ongoing Present.

Else is fastened with knots onto this black soap bubble cosmos in front of the window bars. This dark room wants to threaten Else with its whisper undertow. This secret stock wants to internally frighten Else out of her wits. This great wall wants to lop off a Hans and an Erika. That Else has no thought hanging over the boundary of her body. That Else has everything stuffed back into the taut paunch. So that Else is not able to go out in her heart to her HansIloveyou. Cannot wriggle out into the firmament of heaven on a thread of congealed head chimera. Cannot fly on a memory trapeze in extended movement.

8.   THE DEPARTURE

Else is gone. For the good Hans Else is recent but past. This ridiculous most Recent Past has gone back to the countryside to Mommy and Father. Now Mamma Rinx dominates again. Wherever one can see in kitchen and chamber, a terrible Mrs. Rinx is at work. Decent in Words. She spins her deceitful little threads. She entices pretty paper into the drawers. The sideboard shelves receive decorative lace. Paper lace order is half of life. An unpleasant jerk embroidering such a restored Mrs. Rinx hearkens here. She does not need to rest. Nor resign. She does not want to admit such a thing in her own home sweet home. Neither will she listen. She prefers to feel. She stores potatoes in the pantry. She cooks rice and meat with plenty of red peppers. She scrubs used-up earthenware jars. A durable respectability is cupped by Mrs. Rinx. She should always have a good circulation. There is so much to conduct in this request concert. All these simultaneous times need to be whirled efficiently the honey. There has to be a rapid torpedo into Hans's up rising.

Softlysoftly.

Onto the bier this sick Else horniness, and two candles on the left and on the right. Mrs. Rinx does not have to admit such a thing in her own cozy home. Now Mrs Rinx embroiders with her own fingers with blue thread. *Happiness Alone.* Naturally with lace around the edges. She drapes the antimacassar over the ottoman. Such care finds favour with every man. Something smells a bit of moth balls. It will fade. It is an alleged Past that is supposed to be cast onto the rubbish heap. Mrs. Rinx demonstrates an elastic Present. Flexible like the linoleum under the kitchen table.

Mrs. Rinx operates indolently cooking lips kisses sewing cleaning. Mrs. Rinx drags out her high heels. Her snake skin pumps. The size only just fits. The aged uff power uff revenges uff ash. Pouch. The ovary. Main thing the ankles are slim. And durable. Mrs. Rinx has a little spring on her foundation. A bit of fluff. Mrs. Rinx blows on a few calluses on her hands. She has a Hans under her roof. Hans does not have an Else under the bed clothes. Hans does not have an Else in his sights. In mind. Mrs. Rinx spears her son onto the salver. The scenic presentation. What a charming sight to behold. Mrs. Rinx gazes lovingly at her darling Hans. How wrongheaded a nature sometimes is without help! How helpless a nature sometimes cannot get by without Mrs. Rinx. Mrs. Rinx gladly lends a hand. A Mamma understands the Hans without Words. That is family heaven. Nowhere an Else, who is missing. Who disturbs the harmony of the familial bond. Who shamelessly sticks a foreign leg into a foreign bed. Who dishonours a mother's boy. Mrs. Rinx adds some more vinegar to the salad. That will taste appetizing to her Hans. It will taste sinfully good, the spicy meat tender through and through. It will be a delicacy after this half-cooked casserole. Mrs. Rinx adjusts her stocking seam. Nothing is slovenly in this household. Everything is straight, tidied up, harmonised. The geranium away with it into the garbage. The joyful song in the throat. A little eau de cologne behind the ear. Thus blare the proud sounds of Mrs. Rinx's desire commands. No late departed and no present Mr. Rinx will say, one cannot hear them.

9.   THE GERANIUM

Where is the geranium, says Hans.

The geranium, the geranium, says Mrs. Rinx. I made you rice with meat and plenty of red peppers.

What have you done with Else's geranium, inquires Hans who has just arrived home from work.

Oh, the geranium, says Mrs. Rinx. The geranium withered. What's supposed to become of it. Doesn't it smell good? Take some Parmesan.

Why did you throw away the geranium which belongs to Else, when it does not belong to you at all, inquires the tired Hans who has just come in by the door from his exhausting job.

The geranium is withered. It's not fresh. It's dry and dead and yellowed and dusty. It's almost soil anyway. It's practically as good as pure dust, says Mrs. Rinx. It is dead. So do eat! The rice with meat is your favourite dish. Eat my son.

Hans does not eat. Again Hans does not eat a bite. What is it then with this geranium. It's as if it were bewitched. Mrs. Rinx simply doesn't understand that. Else has gone. The geranium has gone. But the tranquillity isn't there. Hans keeps on asking and carping about a hand full of withered nature. At the same time nature is so rich. Has so many happy hands.

You never could stand Else, maintains Hans, for whom his Mamma makes it so nice at home.

You always made life difficult for Else, Hans has the audacity to say when he is home from work. Notwithstanding Mamma making it as nice as she can in every conceivable way. But Hans eats nothing. He stubbornly stares at the stupid window. Where a stupid imaginary geranium has to be. He stares ahead and eats nothing and only mopes and asks and asks. After each question yet another question. Because the previously so good Hans does not hear an answer. There his Mamma can say what she wants. There the rice with meat can steam ever so fragrantly. Hans is asking on and on and does not hear what his Mamma is saying. Hans pushes away the steaming plate of rice with meat. He only sees an empty space in an empty window. He puts on his jacket. He goes. His Mother, who should be honoured by every household so that it prospers on earth, is air. Out goes Hans, the desired body of Mrs. Rinx, and slams the door shut. Not a chink does this schismatic horrible creature leave open for his dear Mamma. There goes her own breath out into the strange wind. Leaves fury and the ferocious Mamma behind alone. Shoves her into this twilight tomb. Will such a Mrs. Rinx terminate in the midst of her lust for life? Will the bitter musty air lay waste to her?

Mrs. Rinx opens the window. The darkness moves inside. Extinguishes everything that can suffocate her.

10. THE MEMORY

From a prison Else cannot go to her parents. From the marriage prison Else can go back to Mother and Father. In the night black lock-up black heretics hunt. They prowl around Else on velvet paws. Right through Else. Else is sitting in the midst of this entire Word Enclosure of paws. Day and night. Day and night all the key-catch-and bywords rattle down onto Else. Else does not have a clue from where so many Words are supposed to be coming. In Else's head the original and borrowed and adjective and object Words form hideous images. Awful scenes of over life-size acuteness. Else breaks out of the conjugal charnel-house. She overturns the barriers. She boards the local train. Else weeps. At home at the parental table she weeps quite terribly. Else cannot say anything. No Word does Else utter. But she weeps really terribly. Now Else is not a Wedded Wife. Now Else is the child of the parents in the village.

Elsechick don't be like this. We'll start over once more. Begin with wishing from the start again. Don't you know any more that you are a colibri. *Each separate feather extra bright.* Thus Hans Rinx tries to force himself into Else's memory. Hans has come and wants to have Else back again. Hans asks Else's Father for leniency. Else turns over the pages of her memory. *Has each feather of a different colour, not merely like a peacock that has different colours but the same on each feather.*

The trees next to the dance floor sparkle. The lime-trees smell intensely of lime-trees. The wind musicians trill and toot. The wreathed maypole towers up into the black lacquer veneer. In it the starlight twinkles. Else is flying. Hans has an arm on her back. Hans has a hand on which the birdbrain Else is perched, chirping and believing she is flying. Sitting on the bird-lime. Sticking on the lime-twig and thinking that is home. Wrong.

Now Else is at home, with Mother and Father.

Elsechick please don't be like this, come, we'll try again once more. Beginning is more beautiful than ending. You need me, Elsechickcolibri. You unusual creature. Without me as the sun in your cosmos you don't get anywhere. You know how such escaped particles wander around in the world until they are captured by a strong force. They are nothing on their own and don't find any place to stay.

Thus Hans the Poet adores his Else. Hans always precisely knows the world into which an Else retreats. Keeps guard. Hadn't he dismantled it for Else like a bicycle so that Else sees how hopelessly without prospects she is, semiconscious without Hans. Does Else not see how hopelessly she is fading away without Poet and Interpreter and Husband?

So Else slumbers helplessly in her small room. In her single cell. Does not fall asleep out of fear. Out of misery. And never actually wakes up. Because if she wakes up, she is captured and in custody.

But if she *really* wakes up, the spook will be past. *Please.*

You have to come home with me Elsechick, urges Hans. Don't be like this. *Elsechickgorgeous like a sea. That glistens. That rocks me. I see it in your eye.* I will only drink pure water from your hand that doesn't distort my dominant image. Wherever I look, everything is as hard as a diamond. That lacerates my life and my success into shreds. That tears me into pieces so that only crumbs lie around. That is a sword that does not tolerate me anywhere, Elsechickcolibri. That is a female screw with the wrong screw thread.

Hans kneels before Else. Hans presses into her memory filing cabinet. Hans pounds on the early archive. *Eternal Silence gazes at me, you blue sea eye.* Elsechickgorgeous deludes a brain Else with a magnificent image. A *Past* performs itself in the prison like a momentary wedding march. Else in white on the arm of Hans, and Mother Rinx. And Erika and Karl Runk with Mother. And a bouquet of blossoms for the registry office. And a shower of rain for the blessing of children. On foot through the puddles to the wedding breakfast. And a ray of rapture from the outside world into the inside world and back. What sort of a HansTheGlance has Else indeed conjured into her empty life by magic! How indeed will Else prance around in her seventh heaven with her HansTheGlance. Else will remain for her best HansTheGlance the bastion of light. Will resound. Will take the harshest falsetto for a base bed.

An Ave Maria rings out in Else's hesitating ear. A blaring Salve Regina resounds in her nervous security. An irritating thorn bush whirs in the hearing whorl. That goes through and through Else. That goes under Else's clothes which only Hans can read. The ring on her finger closes tightly around her chest. Yes. Hans is to bring the anxiety to an end. The loss of speech will unbind itself with a Word from Hans.

No more Hans who encroaches with his hand. No Hans who languishes close by Else and feeds from Else's hand. No Hans who takes hold of an Else so that she exists in the world. So that she waves from out of the prison. So that she somehow derails on a bodily stream of thought to Hans up there in the clouds.

11. THE FATHER

Good Father benevolent one how right you are with a Good Future at the side of a good HansTheGlance for your Else!

Darling, rustling queen of my future glances, how we swim through the ocean in the big world that our Love is awesome in its greatness that can have nothing more under the stars because we are the most beautiful what I have and what you, Elsiebabefairy can have in absolute devotion. Ek. Yours forever!

Thus Erika hammers into the reconciliation scene. Erika forges so that the sparks fly. Erika forges that there must be bending under the heat and glow. Erika hastens between hammer and anvil. The verse! Is it ready? Is it good? Does it have barbs? Does it cut Else with a scythe?

Good Father gracious benevolent one, the good Woman is not subordinate without her Hansasalways! There is no good ruling over the Woman without a Wedded Husband.

Dear Elsiebabefairy dearest what an intoxication rushes into my senses with a passion without deliberation and chant, and how it roves in all thoughts in sharp showers that I'll never let you go as you now will not get away from me in the Greatest Love, whether you would like it or not, which you are never able to do. Ek. Eternally.

Thus Erika rams her reminders into the marriage settlement. Erika drums into and beats black and blue with all her dexterity. Erika threshes so that the chaff separates from border and grain. Erika flails so that the facts fly out of reality. Erika works bathed in sweat. With blunt force she pounds a little grain of truth out of the Master's verbose Word Mills.

If Erika had not merely reached into Else's firmly welded mass shield. If Erika had only taken this congealed sinter as a warning sign that one does not take hold of. Can Erika not then understand an aggregate state on which one does not fumble around on with fingers?

Good Father benevolent one, the good Wife is subject to her good Husband. And even if for the good Wife being subject would be death.

Chapter Two

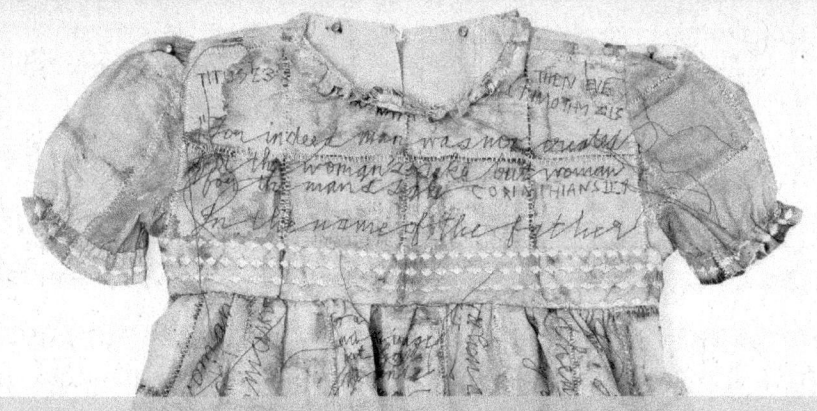

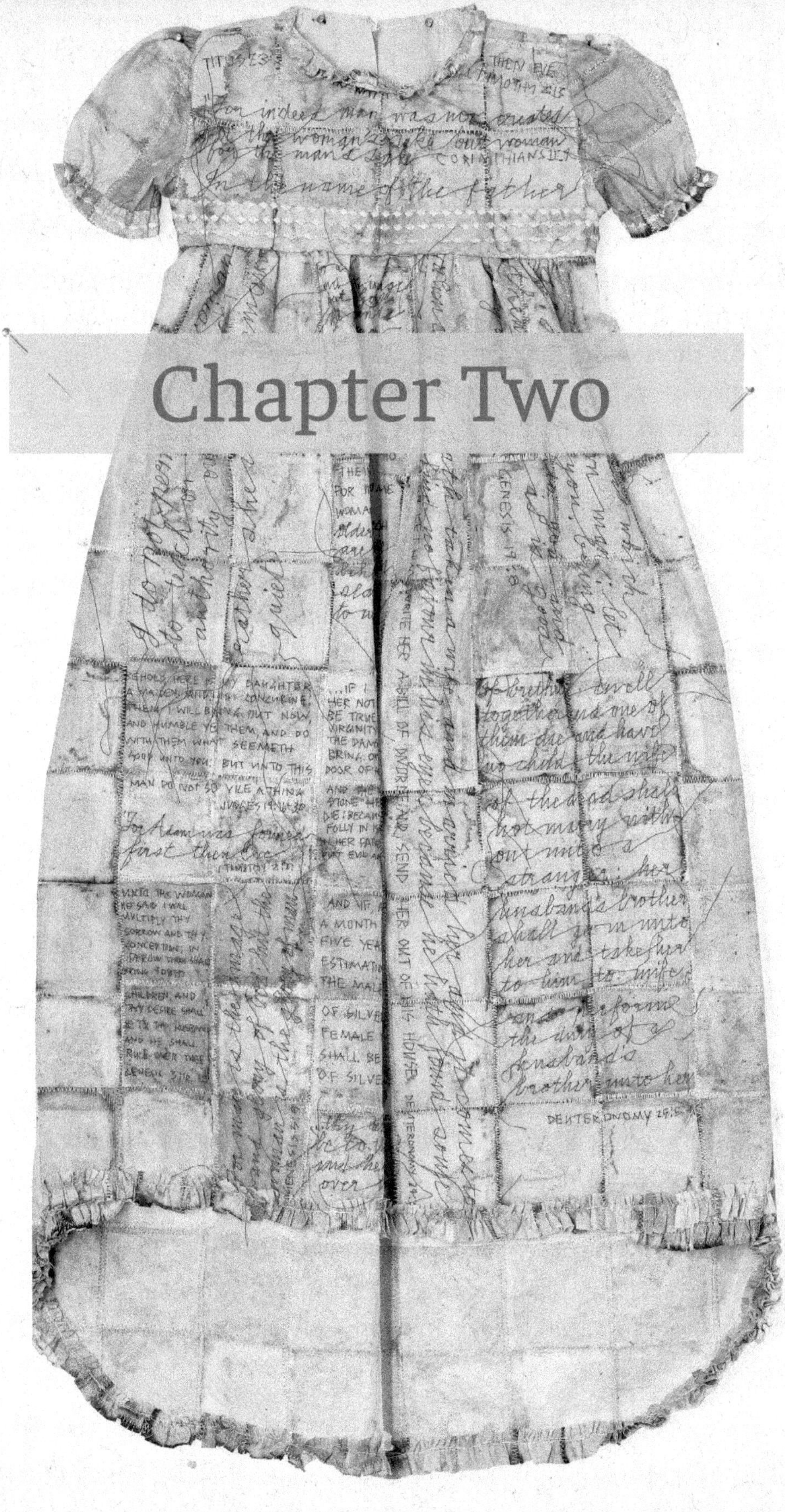
For indeed man was not created for the woman's sake but woman for the man's sake
CORINTHIANS
In the name of the father
GENESIS
DEUTERONOMY

1.   THE RETURN

Mrs. Rinx procures a new geranium. For Else Mrs. Rinx has to buy a fresh flower pot. Else is coming back again. Such rotten luck. Hans is threatening his Mamma. Hans is not very explicit. That isn't necessary. Mrs. Rinx understands her son. Without Words. He is, after all, her product. Even if Mrs. Rinx sometimes doesn't understand him at all. Mrs. Rinx buys a geranium with three pink blossoms. She places the blooming geranium on the window sill. Mrs. Rinx places herself behind the geranium at the window. She is the reception committee. Mrs. Rinx is the brass-band which will strike up a harmony for the arriving Else. She sends her desire vault extra deep down. She seals it up extra solidly. But it is not cleared out. All is not yet lost! On the cooking stove in the frying pan a schnitzel is twittering. Intoned by Mrs. Rinx. A green salad reclines saucily in the salad bowl. Animated by Mrs. Rinx. In the small glass bowl the red berry compote shouts for joy. It boasts. Specially by Mrs. Rinx. A conversion is supposed to take up residence with Mrs. Rinx. She is practically forced into it. Else will not be able to complain about the marching up. Will not be able to grumble about the interior decoration. Festive. And yet mother-in-law-like reserved. Else will not be able to scold about the well-behaved reserve. Hans will praise his Mamma. He will take delight in the arrangements. A well-oiled household proclaims stability to Mamma Rinx. It proclaims stability to Else. Stop, says the household, I am your support. Continue, says the good Hans when he comes home from work. Carry on. Where is my food? Where is the newspaper? So that the communication in the household is smoothly regulated. With radar traps and spring traps. (S)he who lets h(im)erself be caught will be punished. Mrs. Rinx has frozen her legitimate entitlements. In a deep freeze drawer lie the sealed in desires. Here they will keep for a while. For a long boring while, Mrs. Rinx knows. Mrs. Rinx is used to waiting after all. For the late departed Mr. Rinx, Mrs. Rinx had waited in all life bed positions. On the table the red-checked table cloth is lying. The Runx's Erika skips in through the door every fifteen minutes, if Else is here already. In the flower-pot on the table are African Violets from Erika. Like an affliction Erika shoots into the homogeneity. Like a bolt of lightning Erika splits the smooth wave surface. She will yet muddle up everything. She is not the first voice at the return. No Wedded Wife has a Girlfriend at the prominent place. There she has a Wedded Husband. A future, a present or a late departed one. Mrs. Rinx stands at the unsheathing of the sword. She has to wait for Else. She has to make a gift of an apple. An enemy incarnation is coming back. This distorting mirror has not allowed itself to be smashed. The picture-puzzle maintains its place. Mrs. Rinx tows the life's destiny barge of the son Hans. She drags it back into the Rinx living room. Mrs. Rinx is the rudder galleon figure of her good Hans. She capitulates. The high heel shoes are back in the cupboard again. The widow's weeds are all around Mrs. Rinx. They ingest Mrs. Rinx.

There Else turns the corner into the street. There Else carries her suitcase. There Else looks up at the window of the lead-grey house. There Else sees Mrs. Rinx. There Else's courage sinks. Thus the old and the young Mrs. Rinx sing a round that does not want to rhyme. They fall silent.

2.   THE WORK AND THE HOUSE WORK

Now Hans works as if greased. The exchange of goods functions without complaint. The Hans exchanges one piece of goods for the Else. The Else exchanges a higher good for the Hans. Mamma Rinx exchanges a rights reserved for the good Else. Thus the goods trains circle between kitchen, common room and cabinet. The meagre carriages and the catapult vehicles circulate. Reject goods and sugar water course from person to person. Else's most precious gift is naturally expensive. Hans pays in biological natural produce. As long as Hans has sufficient ready. As long as the wreath on the maypole tilts up and down. Then Hans pays in the customary currency, in valid bank notes for the household expenses. Thus the coniferous forest of the public economy is intimately bound up with the private maypole of Hans Rinx. For an Else Hans is worth more than a garden and castle together. More than jewels stars stockings. The familial added value of the Hans is considerable. He raises the nutritional value. Hans derives it from his potency. Explosive power. A Hans Rinx is capable of exploding at home at any time. That results in protuberance! At the factory he then he becomes a cog in the works. The colourful ribbons of power and value added flutter around Hans and every report. Hans the bogy is tied up in this glowing bow by Mamma Rinx and Else. Hans comes home from work. He places the aureola in the centre of the kitchen. Else and Mamma Rinx kneel before it and demonstrate their devotion. Then they fetch polishing cloth and wax and rub and wipe and polish and varnish it. The Hero of the Day is eating his supper meanwhile. A bird brain Else has to pay instalments for a long time until this happy destiny is paid off. The bird brain Else is left to guess for a long time how things are in Hans's world. The bird brain Else is not supposed to arrive at the idea that he himself would like to have a halo. Otherwise an obstruction comes into the exchange of thought goods than can extend into the public conveniences. The intercourse of the world! In this escalation of goods Else is not able to compete either. There something more precious than Else's most precious possession is at stake. The bird brain Else does not even suspect it.

Hans has eaten well at supper. Mrs. Rinx has sat there quietly for the whole long evening. Else is here again. Hurrah! Hans takes a tot of spirits in celebration of the day. In a water glass so that Else does not notice it. There is a request concert in the House of Rinx today. Else does not forget that she belongs to the private household equipment of the Wedded Husband Hans Rinx. To his movable property. Mrs. Rinx hears a Requiem in her inner ear. If it is supposed to be a lament for a woman dead in the Widow Rinx? Or has Mrs. Rinx played out? There is a lot of minor in Mrs. Rinx today. Today Mrs. Rinx is a silent character. She hears a Requiescat in her head. Hans is at the pinnacle of pampering. Hans tingles in a twilight and in all variations. Hans is fanfare and hunting horn. He entices the animals into the forest. Else is transfigured. What a show! All just for Else alone. Such a return is an event. It is crossing a bridge and a spreading the tail. A triple somersault on the trapeze without a safety net. From the morning to the evening. Up until the night.

At the window a new geranium is standing. It has three pink blossoms. The old one has disappeared, Else sees. The half-dead one by means of which Else telegraphed with Erika. Else will not speak with Erika any more. Hans is right as always. The dear good HansTheGlance. Else will not exchange a word with Erika. Not a syllable. Not a wink and not a look will Else exchange with Erika any more. Erika is a sphere. She is a thoroughly bad influence. Erika is smitten with every breeze. Erika spikes a fire. She does not even know it. Erika spits pestilence from her pores. No-one catches scent of that straight away. So dangerous is Erika the absolutely leprous. Else sees it clearly and sharply. When she once sees it with the eyes of the good HansTheGlance. There the dear good HansTheGlance is quite right. Erika is a culpable monster with a cleft double pincer. A barb-tongued monster Erika is greedy for possession. Dried up. Desiccated. A wilted meadow is Erika, who does not bed any Wedded Husband well. No man at all can deliver for Erika. Straighten.

Everyone sees what Erika has caused in the marriage of Hans and Else. Erika tramples through the tender sylvan glades of a young marriage so that the delicate seedlings of a young love take dreadful fright. She destroys growth with her blubbering. How can Else have a Girlfriend Erika! Such a rotten rock. A fistula a ferrule in her entire fearlessness. Two hundred and twelve degrees Fahrenheit of greenhorn.

Hans glances around carefully at his happy event Else. She will tremble violently under the heat of the reading. The glow of the gesture under the cover burns a track. A groove emits a tone. Thus speech comes into Else and sets Else in motion. Else is moved by all the charming Words of her good dear HansTheGlance. She feels so hot from unadulterated expectation. From unadulterated promise. The good dear HansTheGlance keeps all promises. He only drinks water. Hans drinks one glass after the other this evening. Hans is no animal. The animals have all been enticed into the forest. Soon it will become cooler. Soon Else will sleep.

3. THE MARRIAGE

Else is living at last! Else is living! In the Marriage it is as torrid as in a romance novel. Such a Husband pays housekeeping money. With the housekeeping money Else buys the world. 1 chrome frying pan 1 knife block pure wood 1 glass fruit bowl white with pink glass blossoms 1 scatter cushion with appliquéd roses pink 2 brushes turquoise one always needs 2 pink plastic basins one can always use, too 1 decorative watering can copper-coloured. Simply like that Else shops. So grand does a Married Woman have it. Now Else is an Element in the World. But only one of them. Else sings and irons. Else warbles and cooks. Else chirps and wipes. Wall and calf and doyly. Else polishes and peeps. And flutes and fiddles and threads the needle. Else coos in the crockery. Else chirps and pays the electricity bill. Else is somehow joyful and all that. Else blares during the day like a butterfly. She moves the cupboards and scrubs the backs. It is happiness for Else. All around Else there is a good State of Marriage. With funfares in her room. Candy-floss sparklers and advent hymns It may be the tiniest space in a hut but just for you and me. An owner counts on it. Hans conveys Else away from the public interest. That is his home work. Else drops into a boudoir where Hans can catch his wind. That is her vocation in nature. Nature has written that with invisible ink, black on white. Even if Else sometimes is not able to read it. Else advances the economy with her little red household strings. So that public and private are continuously confused. A Married Woman simply whispers differently. She clears the crumbs off the table. Else strokes the red and white table cloth smooth. Else takes care. Of everything. Mother Rinx crumbles away in the dump. Else patches shirts. Else does not need integral calculus. Who needs that anyway. Else is an integral stock of the Rinx fortune. She is able to refurbish every yawning abyss. Else mends socks, too. History and natural history are not necessary for Else. Else is nature in its purest form. A torrid torrent who makes up a bed for Hans. Else as a Married Woman is able to roll up skeins of wool. She can embroider rows of button holes. Else can spice something with cardamom. Sews on decorative borders. Stuffs chicken breasts. English is bad for Else. All around the lead-grey house is Germany after all. Up to the borders which Else does not see. Where is she to speak English? For inside the private marriage Else capably keeps house. That is nobody else's business, outside. Reading is nothing at all for a Wedded Wife. It confuses Else's thinking. Else puts turmeric in the turkey. Is something like that right? Else is an extremely happy Wedded Wife. Leads a splendid life in the fenced-in Circle Suburb. There Else can go around and around. For a long time. There is always a palisade fence there. Protecting the tariff area from the free enforcement of wishes. Else can be glad that she does not earn anything. What sort of liabilities and expenses she would have. And taxes. Else would have to pay for a charwoman, a washing machine, a dish washer, a house keeper, a seamstress, a cook, a stoker, house painter, glazier and the whole long list. Else is glad and all that. Else is a user-friendly Service Centre. As such, Else can be really glad. Interest is low with this tender. Else takes on every task. To general satisfaction. Else, of course, has high ideals. Money is spoken about only by men behind closed doors. It is disgusting. A leading man is not scared of anything. Not even of enormous sums of money. Else would die of fright there. There one has to be trained for a long time so that it becomes a habit. Else is in the delightfully non-utilitarian household. There is no nasty money in there. That is at most in the intoxication of the shopping frenzy at the department stores. At the baker. At the butcher. At the hairdresser. At the hosiery shop. In the knitwear hall. A household has what there is. There is never enough money. There is Else. Else begs Hans for more housekeeping money. Hans refuses. A Marriage is something private. An immaculate place. There is no paying there. Money does not belong in his home. Hans is right. It belongs in circulation. This gondola arrives where Hans works perfunctorily. Hans sends the gondola on to the market coterie. It makes a stop at every pillar of the market economy. Boom or bust. Continues swinging always oscillating in this venerable horrible male bravery. Else shudders when Hans tells of that. In Else only Hans booms or bites. Else is glad and happy and all that.

4. THE PARISH FAIR

Hans Rinx brings Karl Runk home with him from work. Hans and Else and Karl and Erika go dancing. It is May again. There are the colourful ribbons on the maypole. There are the lime-tree blossoms with the scent. The brass-band is there. Everything is as it was last year. Almost everything. Karl and Erika were not there. Else was still with her parents. Three hundred days with Hans were not past. And with his mother Mrs. Rinx. Three hundred days in the lead-grey house were not past. Days as heavy as lead. The Ardent Telegramme Method in Love was not there yet. No geranium transmitted a Morse dialogue to Erika Runk. No torments were there. No performances by Mamma Rinx. No nymph scenes. Everything is well-concealed in a Good Future. In an unjust Future. Else will not think about that today. The evening is so beautiful. The sky is so velvet blue. And Erika is merry with Karl. Hans says Elsechickseablue, everything is as it was. Elsechickseablue, you course though my thoughts like warm blood. Hans talks like this. He drinks only pure water. A feverishly hot source from inside are you Elsecolibri, says Hans. You will burn me up internally. You will glow red-hot through my guts. Elsechickcolibri you wreath my mind in mist. This is how Hans gets underway. Erika barely glances at Else, the air, not even there. Does not give Else any message folded up tiny. That singes a hand. Erika only sees her guy Karl. And fizzes signals and sparkles. Erik is a changed person this May. That is something completely different, of course, says Hans. Married Couples go out with Married Couples. Correct. Hans is talkative today. Karl laughs. That is the sound of the world. Married Couples are not any Single Persons. Internally a Married Couple is a spinning-top. A confusion for conceiving children. That is a turbulence behind which something wants to get hidden. But there is nothing set behind the surface.

A well-known story about a crocodile. A Married Couple is one heart. That is the hammer that the Wife fabricates. And a meaning. That is the anvil of the senses, says Hans, who simply just knows it. A Married Couple is very private. Nothing comes in. Nothing is allowed out. That is written by providence. That stands in the passport. The good dear HansTheGlance removes Else's fear of Erika. Erika is now the path on which Karl tramples around the World. Karl is a few intensities of current more and Erika is the nobody in this noose without end. That is something completely different. That nullifies all prohibitions from Else to Erika. On the contrary. A Married Couple is the best insurance company. The best business. Against the light Else sees how right everything is. Nowhere a brute in sight. Nowhere a residue. Elsechickcolibri, somehow you have grown. You are a nothingness that does not quite vindicate itself. Evaporates. Now you are the condensed water that forms on my forehead, Elsechickgorgeousyou. Mild is the May air in which Else lives. The lead-grey house is far away. A merry mood is in the married couples. Erika shouts for joy. Erika hops high. Karl nips Erika in the hip-bone. Erika shouts with joy. Karl pinches Erika on the cheek-bone. Karl is affectionate toward Erika all round. Erika appreciates that. Hans and Karl drink only pure water. They are Married Men, of course. Hans glows rather red in the face. Karl is a dark red lamp. Other people smell strongly of spirits. That one could think it could be Hans. That one could think Hans and Karl are exhaling fumes. But that cannot be so. Else does not think of that now. Else drinks a fizzy cool drink. She takes a draw on Hans's cigarette. She splutters. Erika laughs. Erika takes a draw, too. Erika splutters, too. Karl and Hans guffaw over such sweet women. Hans starts wanting to go home. Else does not want to. Karl slowly starts wanting to go home, too. Erika wants to stay. Must carry on! Everything must carry on like this!! So wonderfully fine like the membrane onto which they are all harnessed. It is thin. It rips easily. If one looks there. Blood flows. It is death. It is a float.

It is a knacker. Time flies a shard gone astray. Stop. Everything is turning around. Else feels dizzy. The ribbons of the maypole wreath above fly gaily past the eyes. Turning and turning. Hans holds Else. Hans stops the swaying loops in Else's head. Thank you. Carry on. Erika wants to dance. Carry on. Erika wants to swing her ankles. Carryoncarryon. Not stop now. Not for anything.

5.   THE LAUGHTER

Else giggles and gurgles. Else laughs and cackles and peeps. Else fizzes and gushes and twirls. Hans supports Else. Else must not fall over from enjoyment. She must not die from fun. Hans drains the bottomless Else. His unfathomable Wedded Wife needs a fortification. Else finds Erika so funny. Erika jumped, laughs Else. Hans holds her. Erika hopped and wagged her head, Else bubbles over. Else almost cracks up. Hans holds her. Haha Erika sprinted across the dance floor with her nose high in the air, Else bursts out laughing and buckles at the knees. Hans props her up. Erika hahaha wriggled on her knee caps over the dance haha floor and hehe her teeth haha, hehes Else and claps on her wrist. Hans floors Else. It is done just like that. Straight away this cackle female is expedited into lead-grey custody. Straight away this giggle nest is again brought into line with the strict pattern of order. Into the spare corridors of discipline. Hans unlocks the apartment door. Else has to be noiseless. Quiet, otherwise Else will wake Mother. Else whinnies and bleats and hisses and puffs and bends over and holds herself and squirts tears and writhes and shrieks with laughter. Hans is irritated. Something floods over all borders. Dangerously the laugh stream overflows the signposts. Something will happen if Else does not stop. Else does not hear. Else, begs Hans, hold your tongue, control yourself, Stop! Else does not hear any voice of Hans. Else's thinking constructs a gun turret tent of merriment for her. This unsurpassed ridiculous Erika! This entangled intelligence root dwarf trollip well in drought-stricken steppe leaky to boot, too. Licks Karl's toes and feet. Wheedles and drools and apes around and makes a fool of herself. Begs fawning for kicks and twines around each one with garland and kiss. It is Erika's communion with her Lord and Master. A kick into the state of grace of the Wedded Wife. Into the intimate elevated life of a domestic animal. That is completely private and nobody else's business. Else takes a deep breath for a new laugh missile. Else gasps air for a shrill salvo of laughter. Hans is shocked. Else has not ever been so terribly threatening! Hans is frightened. Hans does not understand what is going on with Else. Else is out of hand. Hans loses his patience. Hans is dexterous. He corners and coralls Else. He gives her a mighty box on the ears. Else comes to a halt. Else is struck dumb. A few tears flow from Else's eyes. A rage a thirst for revenge a murder a cunning attack glows on its foundation. Hans does not know why. Else does not know why either. Else flares up at Hans.

There is a frenzy in Else. A boiling up a ferment an agitation. Now the laughter whirls around in Else. Turns Else around and around. Beneath the skin the wild waves collide with a strict prohibition. Roll back inwardly. Gather strength. In Else they continue growing. Swell gigantically. Splash over a contour. Obliterate a clear picture. Else grabs Hans by the collar. Else shakes him by the lapels. Else punches the whole bag. Else has gone mad. She is laying violent hands on a Wedded Husband. She is striking against Hans's garment! At last Hans recovers from the surprise. He grabs back into his Wife's hair. So the Married Couple tear and tug at one another. Between table and refrigerator. Hans has already garnered several tufts. Else pulls Hans on the sleeve, he labours. Hans presses Else's thumb, there is gurgling. Else claws at the suit jacket. Else scratches Hans's hand. The jacket lining rustles. Onto the floor rattles what was inside it. Keys. Matches. Handkerchief. Comb. Money-purse. Coins.

6. A DOOM

Now suddenly Else is tired. Else sits down. Else wipes over her tired face with her tired hand. Quite suddenly Hans is very tired, too. Hans tiredly crawls on the floor and gathers his things. Else does not receive a box on the ears. Notwithstanding. But Hans is not angry with Else any longer. Else is not outside any longer. In the dangerous laughter tower. Else cuddles with Hans. Into bed. A Married Couple reconciles quickly. They are rapidly really tired. Hans and Else will have to go to sleep early. Else rubs her eyes. Else yawns a little. Else stretches her legs. Straightens her shoulders. On the floor at her chair leg Else sees a photo. Else bends down and picks up the colour photograph. Wants to hold it out to Hans. Else stops short. Her arm stops in its bend. Draws the print closer to her Eyes. Nothing. Else does not see anything that makes sense. Else recognises nothing. No object. Else is puzzled. Focusses more sharply. Sees? Does not know what. A thicket? A dried up meadow? A mound of sand? A muddy field-path? With isolated dry grasses? A cleft rock formation of grey porphyry? Out of leached volcanic rock? Out of monochrome volcanic rock with indistinct stalk growth? On stone? Bristles? Hans sees the slanting shape in Else's hand. Hans falls furiously on Else. Hans tears the picture out of Else's paws. Tugs at the snapshot in Else's Fingers. How that enrages Hans! Hans is completely wild. His face turns to chalk. What is it with Hans, Else is astonished. What is it about Hans with the photo. Else is amazed. Hans is in an uproar. Flares up. Splatters spiky Word gravel. Flies about an Else with the photo in her fingers. Else sees a field-path. Else sees a winter or late autumn. Else sees a nature snapshot. A sun stroke nature close-up. Else sees a sultry aperture. Breaks? Glows. Really does not know what where. Because of such a nothingness and nothingness again is Hans combusting? Spikes high in rage.

Splices a fibrous split cord. Snarls. Because of a high gloss photo? On which the nature of nature is a complete flop? Else does not understand that. Else pecks like a woodpecker into the cowardly oakum stuff to reveal itself. Else peers closely. *But that is of course.* Else scrutinises. *That is of course a horrible.* It shoots through Else like a shot.

Entry Prohibited.

Else stares transfixed at the stone-grey sex of an old woman. At a bloodless block mottled mucous membrane. At individually standing grey barbed wire hairs. Else sees a part of a female body excised by a photographer. A crude slaughter camera shot has butchered itself something bloodless from out of an old woman's body, sees Else. An Epiphany! A comradely camera eye discarded the useless rubbish immediately, sees Else. The inferior stuff for the birds of prey. The useless remainder for the flayer. Away with it. Out of the way! Hocus Pocus. What remains is the focus. The camera sharply scrapes into the shoddily-cut edges, Mother has been completely dissected.

Precisely according to the rules of lighting. Not any screams of pain at all at the prescription of regular aperture.

All blood is drained from Else's face. Else dangles over an abyss worse than death. And rots. And ticks, the decaying carcass.

Hans carries the unconscious Else into the bedroom. Hans covers Else with the woolen blanket. He picks up the photo. He cannot. No he cannot destroy the picture of his origins. The destination of his journey. Nail shut. Cut out with a sickle. A single bled-out association of immediate proximity. The site of his rage is supposed to be sewn up sealed by Hans? A curtain has been rent. A Word has fallen out of a tabernacle. Well then? Hans is the Word. He will climb inside for sure. The only concern is Hans and Power.

Hans has to hallow the Mother Rinx. And not destroy. Not even a photo. That is at Hans's disposal. Hans hides the photo at the back in the refrigerator motor. Over there Else will definitely never find it. Over there it is in safety. Cheers! For the wellbeing of all concerned. Hans gets undressed. Hans gets into bed. Hans is very tired. Hans cannot sleep tonight.

7.   THE SINTER

Else knocks at Erika's door. Else is pale and silent and bleary-eyed from lack of sleep. Mrs. Runk opens the door. Mrs. Runk gets a fright. There is a misfortune at the door and wants to come in. A shadow is projecting into the house and wants to darken.

Erika! calls Mrs. Runk. Come quickly my child. Come Else is waiting.

Erika comes quickly. There is a phantom at the door and wants to fade away. There a shadow darkness reaches into the room of Erika and Mother Runk and wants to starve. Erika takes Else by the arm. Erika leads Else to a chair. A corset at the bottom end of respiration wants to recover its breath please. Erika strokes Else's hair. Over her cheek. Else looks like white stone. Else looks like a rigid rock from which she cannot break out. Which a nature is presently turning into rubble. Erased from firm ground. From a real threshold. Else is breathing heavily. Erika holds her breath. That Else does not shy away. That Else is not gripped by dread. Does not take to her heels corroded into being frightened out of her wits. The state of confusion turning the tightly twisted agitation into dust into madness.

What is wrong Else?

Else lowers her head. Grey-white membranes lie in wait for Else in front of every face. Leather grows decay crabwalks further into Else's field of vision. Darning needle thick bristles poke into both of Else's eyes. So ashen is Else that she cannot be seen in the snow.

Else don't you want to say what's wrong?

Else jerks her head. It is an eternal light trampled to pieces. It is a time-delayed grenade. Grenades. Gouges a shell-hole in a wide radius. Knocks out a memory. Into an essentially deaf techtonic structure it tortures a giant crater. Eclipses a long recollection. Is annihilated in a dam of heat. Forever. Else is a lead-white pale chalk cliff.

Do tell Else.

Else shakes her head. The shaking continues. Else's Body shakes. Else trembles. Else's bottom Lip trembles, too. The Eyelid and the Breath flutter. The Fingers fly. The Eyes dart about hurriedly. Restlessly. Forth flies the gaze. To a place that Erika cannot see. There a crutch taps about and beckons. Such a hellish noise. Such a clattering deafening din. There a value mills over a bridge. A clasp-knife scarifies a freedom frontally to who knows where. Coagulates something creature-like to a great deal of cast-iron. Wants to depart. Leans as a memorial token at the abyss. Screams. And screams. And screams. Entry Prohibited! Else wants to shrink away. Wants to evaporate into nothing.

Just keep cool Else. You're here with me after all.

Else is not screaming any more. Mrs. Runk hastily brings a glass of eggnog. Poor child, says Mrs. Runk. Poor poor child. Else raises a head with bloodshot eyes. With red eyelid rims. Here today gone tomorrow, says Mrs. Runk. Just don't get the horrors, Else. I have no idea. No fear poor child. Then Mrs. Runk returns to her room. Mrs. Runk leaves Erika and Else alone.

Now a flood breaks out from Else. A spring-tide gushes from Else's eyes. Hot, hot tears. A torrent of Words which no-one understands rushes out of Else's Mouth. A hiccup cuts into them. The sniffing stifles them. A powerful nose-blowing distorts them. The Words are not supposed to be any Words that one can hear and repeat.

They are a Radical Change. That has to come out of Else. They are rubble marbles. Should not seethe Else completely. From out of Else a pro- and epilogue sinter slides out. One without adjective Word slime. Internally in Else place is made for a breath. So that Else is able to simply breathe again. Into Erika's hair Else whispers agitatedly. What no-one real is permitted to hear. What always has to be a bricked-up litany. A wall. Guilt and shame are now in Erika's hair. Sin and atonement leak together on Erika's head. What may never leave Else as a Word. That is curled into Erika's hair-do. Erika is a permanent wave of Else. A tint of Else's voice is Erika's latest tone. The alpha hoof in alphabet. Such a poisonous falsetto can the Love be lying beneath Erika's skin.

Erika fetches the pocket handkerchief. She holds it out to Else. Else dabs her face. Erika takes the liqueur glass. She holds it out to Else. Else swallows the liqueur. Else swallows.

But now it's better, says Erika.

Else nods. Else is quiet. Else is a small boil in an established system. Or is Else a small infected compound withing a large unknown hand? Is Else a horrid scab not to be localised in a much too large a world? Is Else moving? Through all snares and traps?

Oh Elsiebabefairy, says Erika. For once. Oh Elsiebabefairy, how good that things are better now. Hans Rinx is only an illusion. A phantom. A repulsive wild boar like my Karl Runk. A load of small-shot. That's what every man is. A load of bulky rubbish for a special institution. Into which the teeth of the excavator will soon bite. A musk-rat, says Else is very nice, too. With its long gnawing incisors for smiling. And a long naked tail for jumping like a kangaroo, says Erika. My Karl Runk, says Erika, lives in the barracks. He sleeps with his crumpets. With guns and with honour. With the Father Land. And close by the locker door. There an image of the enemy is stuck. He looks like a kangaroo. With a long naked tail for jumping.

My Karl sleeps close by it. Your Hans isn't any different.

There a base rises on which Else can stand. There a trapping security net is strung. It sways. It holds. There is a membrane on which Erika can drum. And Else hears.

Oh Elsiebabefairy, says Erika, it's always only about one thing. About honour. It is the domestic shrew. She sows discord in the world of marriage. She is a female sex with a stinking reputation. Everyone hears her making a noise everywhere. In the dregs in the placenta in the vehmic kitchen. She listens eavesdrops at every neighbour. Each and every Karl has her to lose. Hello! Honour! Honour! calls each and every Karl. She only arrives at the last call. Absolutely the last. In this whole binary net a nonentity is caught hanging. She is allowed to hang and heckle. She is allowed to blush in the obituary notice.

Oh Elsiebabefairy, says Erika, you're an abject species. In the middle of looking you lose your character all the time. From your bad name you exploit a right. Can only simply mangle a speech. Clear scratches and other cadavers away from a husband's upgrading. From the exit. This is what a Married Woman has to do. Sponsor. That is the marital duty. My Karl wants to rely on that. Wants to sign for a loan because of it. That is credit that I don't give my Wedded Husband. Karl Runk should gladly bear the cost for that. The interest and the interest on the interest and the whole profit. Your Hans is no different either, Elsiebabefairy.

Erika strokes Else over her hair. Else takes a sip of eggnog. Else is amazed. Erika is not clever after all. What Erika knows about life! How Erika knows her way around the world of marriage! Erika knows what's what. There Else is completely dumbfounded. Not a single Word is scattered in the winds. Not one misfires. Each and every one has been said. Stands there. Runs into Else. Pricks.

Pushes. Comforts.

Makes a whole Else feel light now. How can it do that. What does it do then. Whether a word introduces itself to Else alone, too? Going, says Else. Going Home.

You want to go already, says Erika.

Now Else is able to go home. Now Else must go home. There Else has to think something over.

Here you're at home, Elsiebabefairy, says Erika. At any time and now.

No. Here Erika chats. Else is not at home here. Else goes home. Back into the lead heavy house. Even if the house weighs heavily. It is home. The Words of Hans cannot get into Else. Locked and sealed. Now Else is eager. Armed.

8. GETTING SCENT

Mrs. Rinx has got wind of something. Mrs. Rinx is very careful. She scents a window of opportunity. A free whiff of morning air. A missing note in a widow twilight. The lead-grey house stands sturdily around Else. Else does not stand sturdily as the centre. As the active ingredient. Out goes Else. Else is always going out to Erika. In the mornings, straight after getting up. The whole day no Else is to be seen any more in the marital strong hold. But Mrs. Rinx is here. She emerges from her position of retirement. She noses out into life into the tile the kitchen. Mrs. Rinx commences cooking Hans an evening meal. Which poor Hans does not eat. Poor Hans. His Wedded Wife does not take care of him. Poor Hans boozes. He boozes and boozes quite dreadfully. What is he to do? He comes home. No Else is there. Hans is drunk and does not eat. Mrs. Rinx does not need to cook at all. But she knows that already. Hans is much too drunk. He sits down on the kitchen chair and falls asleep. He opens his mug and dribbles and snores. Fumes reeking of spirits come from his open mouth. Of sour beer and schnapps. And grunts. His face is red. It glistens and sweats. His eyes roll under the eyelids. Edge up there. Roll about here. Rapidly. The schnapps clod Hans sits in his flat. The passed out Hans sits and snores. He does not eat what a Mother cooks for him. He does not hear what a Mother shows him. He does not see what a Mother offers him. From out of the Mother Rinx a woman who enchants her procreation wants to emerge. From out of the Mother Rinx a beloved territorial claim wants to protrude that will make a Hans actually arable. But the good son Hans erects his boundaries in the public house. With a surrounding rock deposit Hans enters the lead-grey house that he does not see. The good Hans is girdled with a blindness. Is it merciful? His eyes see nothing. His cells silently gather dust.

His synapses remain fallow and deaf. Hans paralyzes himself. He expands his catelepsy concentrically out over his household. Hans is a venomous spider. Hans spreads his deadening web. Mamma Rinx no longer has any real joy with her good son. Her good son no longer has any real joy with Mother Rinx. Mrs. Rinx does not know what is going on. Nobody tells her anything. Something is flitting to and fro. Something sharp. A fish-bone. In an hydraulic circle. Else does not look at Hans. Else does not speak with Hans when she is there. A deep trench runs between Hans and Else. There is a chasm that has robbed Hans of speech. It robs Hans of recollection. Mother Rinx gropes high and low in her quest. Where is the malicious crater? With what is Else torturing poor Hans? Hurls scraps that Mother Rinx can neither hear nor see. Snap! She wants to grab it. And does not catch any edge. Mamma Rinx does not catch any footstep of the dyed in the wool flickering drummer.

9.   THE WELFARE

Else comes back from Erika. Mother Rinx is on the look out. But now Hans will show her something. A hammer round dance. Not on your life!

Nothing to say?

Now Hans will rule the roost. Now Hans will wreak havoc with Else. Will do a little rolling out and stamping. Will do a little pounding and smacking. Will do a little stamping down and knocking and punching. Whacking thumping whipping bruising clubbing. Now Mamma Rinx is really waiting with bated breath.

Hans blinks. Hans closes his eyes.

Has he perhaps not seen his Spouse?

Hansmyson, says Mother Rinx, your Wife has arrived.

Hans's eyelids quiver. Hans does not open his eyes.

Hansmyson, Else is here, your Else has once again found her way home, insists Mrs. Rinx.

Hans does not want to listen.

Hans! Mrs. Rinx has to become somewhat louder, mygoodHansmyson! Your Wedded Property is in the room with us. Feels free to come home late at night. When decent folk are sleeping.

Shut your trap, says Hans to his Mother. Shut your trap and concern yourself with your own stuff.

This is how ungrateful sons are. This is how they repay the Mother Rinx for her eternal care. Hit the Mother with a back stab. Use a Mother as a buffer past the culprit. Takes a detour around the Spouse into consideration. Mrs. Rinx does not know either. Mrs. Rinx does know precisely that everything does not tally here. Here an unreasonable reciprocity is at work. Here a principle has got muddled. Here a Spouse does not force herself. No Duty. That is against the founding principle of the marriage with a Hans Rinx. That should be impaled, quartered executed by firing squad. In this moral code Mrs. Rinx is sure of herself completely and utterly sure. Tar and torture. Rod cane ferrule stick against this outbreak of immorality. Whip lash out in every case her Hans Rinx must punish such a distortion. A Wedded Wife does not simply elevate herself. Say what she wants, despite the Husband having the Word. Simply goes out and in and seasons the turkey with coriander. Is something like that right then? Is something like that the permitted to be possible? A decline of chastity? Decorum rules the World of Women. Mrs. Rinx always went to fetch beer for the late departed Mr. Rinx. Mrs. Rinx fetched the pork roast for the late departed Mr. Rinx and new potatoes and sheep's wool socks and ah. She fetched everything for her late departed Mr. Rinx. Need and sex and character. Is that not a disgrace otherwise? A Mrs. Rinx has to surely seriously ask herself. An Else cannot kick over the traces. They are not there so that Else can go in for sport. Side-vault over and wave from the other side. From over there the Married Men's League and Prudish Brotherhood signal stop with flags Halt. Entry only for Male Humanity. Change signals immediately. Notch sign. Secure driving lane together with kerbstone. Cat's eye radio! Lamp filter brigade tooooot! Hazy brain epitaph tooooot! Catch up. Roll up. Chop symbols march! Refresh series of symptoms. Riiight turn! Hobble cancel Else by means of a stamp without delay. Punch! Alarm! Mrs. Rinx hears alarming piercing sounds. It is a case of emergency calling for the entire Hans. A Mother Rinx does not leave her brood in the lurch.

Hans Rinx now wake up at last, Mrs. Rinx wails like a siren. You really have to concern yourself with your Spouse. Family comes first, my son.

Quiet, rattles Hansmyson and squeezes his eyes tightly shut. The air of the speech takes hold of his uvula. A snore trumpet blast breaks out from his mouth. The beer glass rattles on the table.

Hang it Hans enough now! blares Mamma Rinx. You will now on the spot.

There her manufacture slams onto the table with a clenched Fist. Now on the spot her product malfunctions and with an open hand palm drives into the middle of the face of Mother Rinx. Mrs. Rinx emits a howl.

Else, so help me, she demands, your horrible Husband is laying violent hands on his poor old frail Mother the son of a bitch.

Else walks to and fro in the kitchen as if through pure air. She fetches the glass from the sideboard. She takes the milk from the refrigerator. She pours it into the glass. She drinks it up. Rinses the glass. Brushes her teeth. Brushes her hair. Drapes the pink woolen cardigan over the back of the chair. Goes into the bedroom. Closes the door.

Mrs. Rinx withdraws into her bed chamber. She is sobbing and will not be able to sleep.

Hans Rinx steams sweat from his clothes. Hans Rinx snores deeply and dreamlessly. His head is on his forearms. On the table. In the morning he wakes up. Every bone aches. Hans presses the door handle to the bedroom open. He drags Else out from under the bed quilt. He gives her two mighty boxes on the ears. With his fist he hits her on her nasal bone. The bright red blood spurts over the hand of the Master of the House. Hans goes. He sets out for work.

10. THE CLOTHES. THE SONGS.

Else staggers to the wash basin. She moistens the face cloth. She dabs off the blood. The pink geranium at the window signals Message ten. Coming in ten minutes with letter. Erika pushes the curtain aside ten centimeters. Message four. I've a letter for you. There it is already pushing its way through the door. Just now Mrs. Runki's walking past the window.

Alas Elsiebabefairy most beloved Fairy in my Heaven the whole night I've been thinking of you so that I can't sleep from pure boundless passion in a previously empty life thanks to your most magnificent and most beautiful Love of all, which parades in me like an oriental woven fabric while being awake and while sleeping and while dreaming, too. There has been so much youknowalready entered into my apartment with you and when you're here I'll call it by name to you and say it always again and again until madness. Never forget me Elsiebabefairy! Ek.

The nose bleed has stopped. Else puts on the pink jacket. She seats herself at the table. Now Else has to hurry with the letter. Erika writes so beautifully. Never in a million years can Else do that. Else always writes the same. Thank you for the lovely letter. Hans has gone. He hit me. I will come in the afternoon. There will be an hour's time. Your loving Else R. This is how Else writes to Erika. Thank you for the lovely letter. Not able to come. Hans will be coming very soon. Your loving Else R. Or something like that. Thank you for the lovely letter. The Mother-in-law is grumbling! An annoyance. Unfortunately I broke the pretty pink glass jug. Have to darn three socks! Your loving Else. Else quickly still turns the geranium around. Message one. I love you. Else buttons up the pink woolen cardigan. She goes. She runs. She can hardly wait at all. In her a heat wave rises to her head. This is how excited Else is.

Erika is waiting already. Her mother has gone out shopping. Erika twines her arms tightly around Else. Erika is quite red in the face. Else is quite red, too. On her whole body. Quickly Erika and Else slip into the bedroom. Quickly. Mother Runk will soon be back again. Erika and Else slip out of their clothes. Erika and Else slip into bed in knickers and camisoles. They whisper under the quilt. Apple blossom, whispers Erika. Honey flute, whispers Else. Agave top, whispers Erika. Hop waffle, whispers Else. Aorta harp, whispers Erika. Hydrangea hood, whispers Else. Aquamarine ring roll, whispers Erika. Malachite skid. This is how Erika and Else continue whispering. In this and other ways.

Else admires Erika very much. What a lot Erika can do and knows! In her entire life Else has never said so many Words. In her entire life Else has never had so many fine fingers. They can sew and knit and cook and tickle and much more. What sort of a wide world is this Erika Runk! What sort of a tickling titillation is this Erika Runk! Erika is a bed-warm purr. Else's adrenal cortex runs at full speed. Mother faun and monkey orchids in one is Erika Runk! But today the thalamus is chasing the orders through! Each and every tactile organ in Else is wide awake. Each and every stimulating follicle shoots into Else's mind.

Tell nobody that I fondle you, says Erika. Promise, says Else. Tell nobody that I stroke you, says Erika. Promise, says Else. tell nobody that I finger you, says Erika. Promise, says Else. Tell nobody that I kiss you, says Erika. Promise, says Else. Tell nobody that I embrace you, says Erika. Promise, says Else. Tell nobody that I caress you, says Erika. Promise, says Else. Tell nobody where, says Erika. Enough, says Else. I can't any more. Stop, says Else. I have to go shopping now.

There is so much singing in Else's head. A shoot a sprout a stem or something like that. A ramification a sapling a runner or bark or something like that. Something blooming a type of edge of a leaf an umbel or stigma panicle or something like that. Else is a little confused in her head. A whole cloud of Words is available. Else had never noticed anything of it before. A humming of mainly nouns impels its non-opaque game. There is just such whirring. A foliage tree-top buds in the sepal or something like that. It is like beneath the roof of the beribboned maypole or something similar. Else is rather joyful. There is singing out of Else from out of her head. Else can barely keep the voice inside herself. Pollen a filament in the ramification of stalk and stem and sprig and so on shoots out of Else. That has never before happened to Else. Pollen, sings Else, a filament in the. According to the melody of evening it comes into being again. Ramification. One is permitted to sing loudly. Speaking not on the street. Else has bright red cheeks. And a bright red forehead. And bright red ears. Else buys baking powder. Else buys three eggs for an egg dish. Supper for Hans.

11.   THE DROSS

For three days the pork fat has been drying out in the frying pan. Two large flies have suffocated in it. In the thick slime a living fly is stuck. Its legs struggle in the jelly. It buzzes with its wings from time to time. That is a kitchen song. The smallest midge dots dance in the air. A rancid smell rises from the streaks in the pan. Decay steams from the sticky plates on the edge of the sink. A sour thread curls up from out of the salad bowl. Insects drown in the salad vinegar. On the table bread crumbs dry out. In a puddle of apple juice a bloated crumb soaks. Starts to go mouldy on the top. Mrs. Rinx cannot look at such a scene for much longer. There the stomach of a Mrs. Rinx churns. In a corner a heap of smelly laundry is lying. It grows and grows. In height and odour. That does not bother anybody in this household. Mrs. Rinx finds a sock at the foot of the table. She picks it up and adds it on top of the mountain. The refrigerator is empty. Else is not in the flat. Else even not there when Hans comes from work. Mrs. Rinx opens the window. That does not help much. This rot cannot be aired away. Hans does not see it. Hans does not smell it. Hans comes from work. He is barely able to stand on his legs. Hans comes back from work. He can hardly stand upright. Hans comes home. He sags at the knees. He sways. And staggers. Saliva dribbles from out of his mouth. A tongue rolls to and fro in it. Like a snail a tongue creeps around in his mouth. Cannot produce a comprehensible Word. Babbles. Loudly rumbles threatening sounds. Rolls tiredly back on the gums teeth where. Go where Hans cannot go at the moment in the look of his eye. Hans gesticulates and ferments. Hans still has an account to settle. That stands hard. Not like nothing else with Hans. In his agony it is still a motor. It drives a Hans around. Chases him from glass to glass. Shoves him into the lead into the grey house. Eggs him on from the chair in the next flash of the eye. Scares him out into the public house. Where Hans just arrives, Hans is not able to stay. Where Hans just arrives it is not time to knock off work. Where Hans just arrives dread courses through him. He has an account yet to settle. He has to move along immediately. It has to happen on the spot. Hans only does not know exactly what. That will still tear Hans apart. Hans has yet to experience it. It will break Mrs. Rinx's heart. A Mother cannot bear such a misfortune in her only child. There is only one reason for a Mother Rinx's son. Her good son despises all women. Apart from Mamma who is not one. Only a son can be victorious, said the late departed Mr. Rinx. A son alone is champion in a family in a world, said the late departed Mr. Rinx. You will have a son if you please, says the late departed Mr. Rinx to his Spouse. Do not be confined for me with any skirt. A Mrs. Rinx is always a good Spouse. Of course she has a son. That is the only chance for a Mrs. Rinx. There a Mrs. Rinx is permitted for a double life span to wash long under pants and iron men's shirts. After the late departed Mr. Rinx she is permitted to conjure glazed liver with lots of onions and parsley potatoes onto the table for Hans. Polish his shoes. Put up with his crude thrashing for his defeats. A Hans Rinx is always stuck in the middle of a belly flop. A Hans Rinx is always swimming in a drop of absinthe. A Hans Rinx steers a direct course toward an industrial accident. That is in his nature. In his mother nature. Mrs. Rinx is very concerned. She can smell it with her acute instinct. Here something stinks. Here a serious internal conflict is taking place. Here there is an antagonistic clash in her good Hans. That moves as an antagonistic clash into the most inward Mrs. Rinx. Mrs. Rinx does not know how a mother is able to help. A champion is sitting there at the table and slobbering. Wobbling and whining for an Else. Dozes off. Wakes up when Else comes.

Else arrives cheerfully. Else comes humming in at the door. She brings three eggs with her. She prepares scrambled eggs. She whistles and whisks. She warbles and salts and peppers. She whistles and scrapes the scrambled eggs onto a plate. She bleats and sets the plate before Hans. She skips three steps. She is out by the door. Hans sits mute. He shovels the food into himself. Do you want bread, asks Mrs. Rinx. No, grunts Hans. Now Hans does not eat any bread. Hans does not eat the bread from his Mother. There Hans prefers not eat anything. There Hans rather drinks beer. Another one. And yet another one. Until the evening comes to an end. Hans does not show his Spouse who is boss. Mrs. Rinx does not understand that. Hans does not make his Spouse toe the line. Mrs. Rinx cannot comprehend that. Mrs. Rinx has a dreadful sympathy for her son. Mrs. Rinx takes a terrible interest. What kind of magnificent gateway had she brought into the world! What sort of a dictatorial territory had she packed into the family hierarchy! An ear throne. A Geiger authority. A provincial principal in the family stable. Mrs. Rinx had given birth to her club-law. The good Hans will be laced into this corset now! Understood? How, Mrs. Rinx does not yet exactly know. Mrs. Rinx will have to set a slow fuse. Mrs. Rinx will have to puff a little into the smouldering.

Hansmyson, says Mrs. Rinx, don't take it so seriously.

Shut your trap, says Hans to his good Mother.

How you speak to your good Mother, says Mrs. Rinx.

Keep your trap shut, says Hans, otherwise there will be trouble.

You are a little unjust Hansmyson, says Mrs. Rinx. You have to resist, Hansmyheart, a good mother helps her child. You are the Master of the House, taunts Mrs. Rinx.

Shut up! roars Hans. Shut your trap! He slams his fist onto the Table Top. Keep yourself in check you old besom, Hans Rinx blows his good Mother off into the feeling wilderness.

Hans makes the familial live rail incapable of interfering. Rips import and export from the nail. Closes admission and information with a snap. Battens down the hatch. Beer flows solely into his trunk. That is his world! It is wet, high in calories and hazy. It sways a bit. It wobbles a bit. It is absolutely reliable. It consists of a simple image. A bottle of beer. It is the case of precedence in the life of Hans Rinx. Hans Rinx pays for it. In return its performance always stays the same. It creates stability in the world. Never is it at war with Hans. It never sulks. It never holds out a memory to him. Never does it show him a photo that Hans has forever hidden from himself at the back of the refrigerator. It is a curved piece of glass. It holds each and every image. The mirror distortion draws other lines. Anyone is able to look at it. No-one recognises some thing. Hans cannot recognise any thing. Not with the best will in the world. What does it concern Hans what it allegedly is. It is a bottle of good beer.

Mrs. Rinx is in the small room next to the kitchen. Mrs. Rinx is weeping. She will pay Else back for this. Else is to blame. Else is guilty of all the rubbish. She will pay dearly for everything. Cent for cent. Mrs. Rinx does not have a monster son. Else has dug out all the scurf. Has made a crude tanner out of him. A loud lout. Such misery. Mrs. Rinx sobs loudly. A leaky piece of no. No. Mrs. Rinx will not utter the Word. Not for the blood of her spleen. March child. Hans. How the thoughts stumble now in a Mrs. Rinx. Because a Word tripped them up. Jolts around. How then is thought supposed to flow? Each and every one is disabled, which is not mentioned. Only the sniveling in the Mrs. Rinx has no obstructing reasons. On the contrary! Mrs. Rinx wrings her hands. Tears her hair out. Rolls around in the dust and moans. That is a misfortune in the interior four walls of the Rinx family. That is complete ruin that is threatening dreadfully.

12.   THE MESSENGER. THE BEER.

Else wants to say something. Erika wants to say something, too. It does not stand in the letters. It stands hidden behind something. Behind the thoughts. Over there it stands firmly. It has no Words. But it demands something. Urgently. It waits for its appearance. That will be penetrating. Caustic. It hides itself well. Stays still and waits.

Dearest Elsiebabefairy you happy little bird you flutter in the spring sun heaven of my eternal Love for you, which in you warm ray is a miracle without hinterland is a pledge to me that you have to give me for always and I to you inseparably. Yours Ek.

Is Erika a mortal being? Who writes such lovely letters. Who has such beautiful brainwaves? Who drives winged horses through the heavens. So that Else is dazzled by its velocity. So that Else cannot keep up with the reverberation. An Else never writes so quickly. An Else never has such a beautiful imagination. And so many different Words not at all. A glittering foundation. A store house. What is Else there other than a fragment. Else turns the geranium. A quarter turn. Meaning *Thank you. Message received*. It is Message eight in the secret index. Which only Erika and Else can interpret. Message four *I have a letter for you* Erika transmits back in the Morse code. Is Erika a mortal being? Who writes such beautiful poetry? Who nickcl-plates the Words with such flourishes and bows. Not so straightforwardly and insipidly to the point like Else. *I have a letter for yo*u. Already it is pushing inside under the door. Mrs. Runk is outside walking past already. Else transmits back like a carbuncle. *I love you*. Main message signal from Else. Erika wants to read something like that continually. Else knows that precisely. Message one. That is at any time the main work in the life of Erika. The three pink blossoms lick directly over to Erika. That is the chief activity in the life of Erika and Else. The radical curtain. Erika puts on the pretty sky blue waistcoat. With the beautiful tambour embroidery in front worked by herself. In her beautiful waistcoat Erika walks past. Inserts a new lovely letter. One after the other lovely one. In this way a day passes joyously. Each one flies by as happily as every other one. Else flies along, as best she can.

Dearest Elsiebabefairy I worship you shining bright blossom in the formerly quiet chamber of my heart, which connects us on a single straight axis no star disconnects. In our bright longing there is no guarantee, so that you have to give me one at last, otherwise you'll shred this magnificent bond of our hearts eternally and destroy everything that I have and am eternally yours Beloved Ek!

Hans comes, the bothersome circuit breaker. Hans makes a noise in the entrance hall. Hans shuffles along the corridor. Scratches with his finger nails on the door handle. On the endings of Else's nerves. Hans lays the axons bare until Else leaps like a reindeer in lap land. Hans is happy. Who dances loves a Hans Rinx. Who cannot stop a Hans can well be fooled by Hans. *Hans is here*, Else quickly sends Erika the message five. Hans is already coming in at the door. His eye balls are red. His eyes are blood-shot. Shome on in he slurs and laughs. Hahahooch he ho hahaaaha! What kind of a nonsensical laughter is always biting Hans since recently. And all on his own. Nobody is laughing with him. What sort of a human being is coming there. Else does not know either. Where had this person been previously hidden. Else does not know either. He must have already been there in Hans. He had been there with Else under the ribbons of the maypole. And Else had not noticed him. Else had not seen the other shadows. The shadows from the other light that is initially hidden under the bushel. Which everyone conceals behind the bravado in the beginning, if he can. Where did this doppel gänger hide himself? What is he saying when Hans says Elsechickgorgeous. To whom is he listening intently when Hans says *Your gaze is a promise until death*. Where did this forked tongue curl itself up that now can only articulate hehe ho ha hoohooh? Hans slumps clumsily onto a kitchen chair. This kitchen chair clumsy lout. Else despises him. Else turns away and cracks open the eggs. Else cooks Hans scrambled eggs. Hans grumbles and babbles into the air over the table cloth in front of him. This table cloth grumbler and babbler! How Else despises him. How Else resents him. Else bangs down a plate in front of Hans. Else shoves a piece of bread to follow the Plate. Else despises Hans and the plate and the scrambled eggs on it. So deeply does Else despise Hans that her foot does not touch a base. Where Else rubs out there is no longer a base. Where Else extinguishes, over there there is no bush to duck under. Mrs. Rinx is sitting in the kitchen. In the kitchen corner sits Mrs. Rinx and listens intently. Eavesdrops on what is going wrong here. In her black widow's weeds Mrs. Rinx sits and looks at the floor. Not a Word says Mrs. Rinx. Sits in the kitchen and inspects the faulty calculation. Something is missing here. Mrs. Rinx investigates the arithmetical error. Something does not tally. Else does not tally with Hans. Hans does not tally with Mamma. And Mrs. Rinx does not tally with Else. Else is the misstep in the metric foot. The flaw in the weft of this family fabric. Mrs. Rinx sees that quite objectively. Anyone could bet their life on it. Everything deviates in this household. Slinks out by the door. Slips hurriedly into the happy hostile strange world outside. Whether it suits Hans or not. In this fine lace a bobbin is weaving wrong. Breaking the established pattern.

Elshe doo shtay Elsepleashe shtay doo shtayhere Elsheshtay youhoomusht shtaywifmeee. Hans slobbers on and on. Again and again. Hans blethers on and on. Hans drawls out his sentence. Until he falls asleep. Hans does not hear anything else. He does not see anything other than his own lament. But he wants to, if you please! You are the only song in my heart. Else should not grumble of course. And the gutless guitar grumbles. Mrs. Rinx is all eyes. She is on the look out between Hans and Else. Hans talks a whole load of absolute nonsense. He does not find his way out of it. Straddle-legged the Word stands there in whichever footwear. Heavy with miles. Or? Hans staggers away *from that*. Hans staggers off. Takes a turn off into the public house. At home no-one understands him. Here he talks to a wall. It does not believe him in any case. On a stretch of the railroad the domestic goods grow mouldy. Wickedly weighed down in ware houses. Shovel over. All clatter on the same track. Circle. A locomotive whistles. Boooo!

Pfeee! Hans cannot see it at all. Such a confused travelling and whistling and talking at the hearth. Where is the traffic light. Or where is Hans? The eternal light in the transfer of goods. He has gone off in any case.

Else takes the water kettle off the gas. Else pours a glass of chamomile tea. Mrs. Rinx nods off. She dozes on her chair. The inspection does not progress. Mrs. Rinx snores softly in her dream. She is dreaming. Her son is custom made. That is no master piece, says the tailor. It would be best if you put him into a special trigonometric shed. There he will amount to half his size all on his own. That is completely realistic, dreams Mrs. Rinx. Providing him with prongs will not help. Hans has place on a fork as a mouthful. Mrs. Rinx sighs deeply in her sleep.

Else is in bed. She sips her chamomile tea. She hears Mrs. Rinx sighing deeply in the kitchen.

13. THE POISON

Men are a poison in the world, says Erika.

Yes, says Else.

For us women the men are a pernicious poison, says Erika.

Yes, says Else.

Hans is pure poison for you, says Erika.

Yes, says Else.

Karl is a terrible poison for me, too, says Erika.

Yes, says Else.

There's so much unnecessary poison in our lives, says Erika.

Yes, says, Else.

One would have to do something against a poison that is so toxic, says Erika.

Yes, says Else.

One would have to end a poison against the poison, says Erika.

Yes, says Else.

One would have to poison the men so that they can't do any harm, says Erika.

Yes, says Else.

One would have to administer it to them, says Erika. With their food.

Yes, says Else.

Then one would have peace at last, says Erika.

Yes, says Else.

Then we'd be free, says Erika. We two.

Yes, says Else.

You only have to put poison in Hans's food, says Erika.

Yes, says Else.

I must put poison in Karl's food, too, says Erika.

Yes, says Else. Come, we want to do things in the dark.

You procure the poison, says Erika. From the pharmacy.

Come Erika, says Else we'll whisper a little. Littlemonkeytooth.

You go into the pharmacy and ask for rat poison, says Erika.

Oystersteeringwheel, says Else. Oilflashflightturbine.

Listen, says Erika, you must ask for rat poison. That's something nobody will notice.

Abacuscrookedpollenpeg, says Else.

You have to do it to please me. You owe it to me, says Erika.

Appplstemsaw, says Else. Apricotrottingmould. Bear'searshinwrap. Ashtrayhornbark.

Don't be childish, says Erika. Listen to me!

Crazydaisybelltinkle, says Else. Redhotpokerpimple. Broochrhu-barbtobaccoash.

Stop it, says Erika. Do you want me to poison myself?

No, says Else.

Oh yes, says Erika. I'll stab myself in the chest with a poisoned needle. Or with a viper.

No, says Else.

And the poison will flow through my blood and paralyze me, says Erika.

No, says Else.

I'll be dead, says Erika. Or mortally ill least.

No, says Else.

Then wake up, says Erika.

Yes, says Else.

Will you procure the poison? says Erika.

Yes, says Else.

Yes, says Else. Come Erika, I want to tickle you with my tongue in your love tunnel. Come Erika, says Else, I want to slip under your skirt with my hand. Adrenhalinhoneydart. Automobiletyreicebergwine. Else slips. Oh Else, says Erika. Erika begins to pant heavily. Things are going in the direction of Erika's taste. Erika falls into the centre of her enthusiasm. She moans. Else goes through the entire register with Erika. Erika and Else collapse onto the kitchen floor. They roll themselves onto a single level. They moan. They purr. They toss off their clothes in the same coordination. Erika and Else add themselves up. They hook into each other and clutch each other tightly. Just right. This vice holds. Thus is Love.

Will you fetch the rat poison, says Erika, promise.

Yes, says Else. I'm adhering love welts in a particular way.

That'll be our secret performance pledge, says Erika. Groin. Elbow. Fanny.

Yes, says Else.

Our betrothal, says Erika.

Yes, says Else.

Only you and I know that, says Erika. Secrecy is sweet, I say.

Yes, says Else.

The greatest Love has the greatest secret in common, says Erika.

Yes, says Else.

Then we'll be indissolubly connected, says Erika.

Yes, says Else.

Then we are joined by obligation, says Erika.

Yes, says Else.

Will you gulp me up? says Erika.

Yes, says Else.

I'll do the same to you, too says Erika. Together with the dandruff in your hair. Utterly and completely.

Yes, says Else.

Even if we want to, which we'll never want to, we can't ever separate, says Erika.

Yes, says Else. I have to go home now. Mrs. Rinx is already lying in wait for me from the window. Mrs. Rinx will sulk.

Now right away? says Erika.

Yes, says Else.

Quickly say you love me, says Erika.

Yes, says Else.

Else goes.

14.   THE TRANSFORMATION

At home Else is like new. She pulls a stool under the heel-bone for Mrs. Rinx. She cooks a thick kohlrabi soup for Hans. After that there is bacon roasted with potatoes. Else makes a cabbage salad to go with it. Like on Sundays. There Mrs. Rinx can wait a long time for the quarreling today. For a grimace. For an educational event. There she is disheartened. The good Hans tucks in both his legs comfortably under the table. His one head wobbles. Who is bothered by that? Three bottles of beer line themselves up right next to the plate. The bottle opener is already opened wide. A beautiful dense wall of moulded glass is standing on parade. There the good Hans's eyes burn. Is he seeing correctly? Is he in the usual reality. Window there? Yes. Table there? Yes. Own legs under the table? Yes. Oh goodness, the beer glass tips over. It continues tipping in an instant. It disappears. As quickly as Hans looks over there. Where is the instant now? Who knows anything. Hans is not steady. That does not matter. There is Elsechickgorgeousyou already. Rubbing with a rag. Dabbing and dipping. How the home suddenly flickers into beauty and tranquility. What a clapping and clattering in the Heart. Mrs. Rinx places both ankles on Else's stool. She blinks. Here a Mrs. Rinx does not believe something. Where is anything true here? Mrs. Rinx looks keenly once more. She does not see something. Checking is called for. Mrs. Rinx makes an attempt. Mrs. Rinx takes both legs off the wooden stool. Mrs. Rinx goes into her small room. Mrs. Rinx returns with the wall cover from earlier days. She nails it onto the wall. There Else is already looking. Glides up. Else strokes the antimacassar long and broad. Chirps it smooth. The good Hans barely takes notice. Today he is treated with such indulgence. Elsechickgorgeous wipes and jumps to it and cleans. The flat smells of vinegar water. Of sal ammoniac and camphor essence. Else fries and steams and bakes and grills. And cooks thoroughly. And Hans eats. Hans eats eisbein with sauerkraut. Hans eats roast chicken with french fries. Hans eats meat loaf with potato balls. Hans gladly eats butter schnitzel with potato dumplings. And vanilla pudding. And cherry preserve. And green blancmange. And poached plums. Hans does not care so much for dessert. Hans swallows his hops. Hans stimulates his digestion. He drinks one tot of schnapps after the other. That stimulates Hans from top to bottom. Through and through. Mrs. Rinx puts her widow's weeds away in the wardrobe. Widows are only in winter. Mrs. Rinx bleaches her grey hair. Peroxide blonde is summer milk. Mrs. Rinx fetches the snake skin pumps. Else scurries for the shoe cleaning kit. Else does not slack. She polishes the snake scales in a flash. Else gets peroxide blonde hair, too. So that she can pose as a Mrs. Rinx at last. When it comes to a performance which is the same thing to the good Hans. It is all the same to him. Main thing he has a Mrs. Rinx hooked up. So that the train can finally depart. Let off steam, toot! Twee! The train of breaths goes in and out with the good HansTheGlance. A Time table exists. All will be well. Everything but everything will be good.

15.   A REPETITION

Very soon everything is not new anymore. Hans is already so well-known, not only to the Else. Mrs. Rinx is a known quantity to an Erika, a Mrs. Runk and many others like Karl and Hans. What can yet happen when they all know one another? What can yet change when in every individual an image of Hans is firmly inscribed? A shorthand lashed down securely. Else has firmly installed the geranium at the Window set on Message one. *I love you* the pink blossom spoons outuninterruptedly through the window. There Erika gushes out her manifold feelings in Thanks and Love. These flow in letters which fly to Else. Only when Else is with Erika does the rill flow juicily directly into Else. Apart from being with Erika, Else has only been at the pharmacy recently. To purchase Hydrogen Super Peroxide for a beautiful tint. Bleach. Mrs. Rinx is smitten with it. Up to the top. Day by Day. Night by Night Mrs. Rinx puts nothing on. Without putting anything on she arrives at the bedroom of Hans and Else. That does not do anything to an Else any more. Hans does not do anything either. Hans snores and bloats in his bed. Hans is hoisted very high in a cramp by an invisible crane. Hans writhes. He stares with open eyes. But he does not see any Mrs. Rinx. No Else. Hans sees a fright. An oppressive black shadow is a fright that Hans sees. Such festering black suffocating vapours tug at Hans. Internally tear the intestines apart. The organs. The flood vessels. Rip apart the Lung vesicles in little pops. The neuron railway tracks shift onto the wrong point. That is a coal black confusion and collision in this ominous internal tunnel. The dendrites gnaw. Take care! Complete overload! Hans yelps as Hans does. A swampy dark panorama is his reason for panic. His pangs travel like poison shipments to and fro internally in Hans. Cut. And weld cold. Spurt with blue flames. And scatter. Hans cringes and twists in this night mare unfit to march. No stopping off at any Floor of the fright. No orientation in these internal levels and corridors. What kind of corroding lifts jolt over which stubborn stories. What sort of piercing torture stabs through the internal map of the terrain.

Mrs. Rinx stretches leg and breast and arm. None of that projects into Hans's eye. Else is sleeping after all. Or will soon be sleeping. Indefatigably Mrs. Rinx does gymnastics through the marital bedroom of Else and Hans. Who is actually warning whom here? Is nobody at home here? Is Mrs. Rinx air yet again? And knows nothing about it as so often in the life of the late departed Mr. Rinx. In which Mrs. Rinx did not know when it was her turn. When she was genuinely present. Is Mrs. Rinx yet again making too little noise? Hans is noisy. He is making a terrible noise today. He grunts and screams. He twists and bawls and whimpers. Storms and retches. Mrs. Rinx does not understand that. Hans is travelling on another track. In some sort of chamber of horrors. How Else can sleep through this? Or is Else just pretending? Mrs. Rinx does not allow herself to be outdone. Miiiidniiiight, Mrs. Rinx blares into this chaos. She is not going to be cheated today. For twelve cling clang strokes of the clock, Mrs. Rinx pushes against an incomprehensible superior power. Nobody beside Mrs. Rinx is deeply stirred. Else is breathing deeply and regularly. Hans moans and writhes in pain. Mrs. Rinx can hardly believe that. But that is really incredible! Mrs. Rinx is so deeply disappointed, someone in the world will yet pay for that. And, specifically in this world. Which would seem to like to be so unjust to a Mrs. Rinx a whole life long. Even if Mrs. Rinx had not done anything to it.

16. THE POST

Darling Elsiebabefairy, beloved treasure, Erika writes in the morning.

Early in the morning Erika writes, beloved Elsiebabefairy belonging to me alone, are you continually thinking of me, too as I do of you?

Oh Elsiebabefairy, you haven't written to me today! Write because I'll otherwise have to think Love is over, writes Erika a little after the beginning of the morning.

Don't you believe how madly I love you, Elsiebabefairy? Don't you know that you're my breath!? That I suffocate without you, I worship you, Elsiebabefairy!, writes Erika when the morning has barely begun its course.

How must I prove, dearest, how boundlessly I love you and how insanely I suffer when you don't answer, Elsiebabefairy golden treasure, writes Erika toward mid-morning.

The shadow is over and away past the middle of the morning and Erika writes, oh Elsiebabefairy, don't drive me to desperation. I haven't heard anything from you, although it's ten thirty already and you're surely awake Elsiebabefairy! What must I do for you not to torture me so cruelly? I do everything for you Elsiebabefairy you Heaven of my days.

The morning wanders on toward midday and Erika writes, if you don't speak with me on the spot, then I'll do something to myself. I'll go to the zoo! Into the snake pit!

What kind of garden of paradise the snakes must have compared with the torments of hell, into which you push me with your silence. You only keep on saying *I love you*! with the geranium, but that isn't enough as you well know, writes Erika, before she puts the midday meal to cook on the stove.

After she's washed the dishes from lunch, Erika writes, here you have proof of my Love which you expect, so that you finally release me from the torture of your silence. I think only of you in every minute that passes.

What must I still do, Elsiebabefairy so that you finally take pity, you cruel one, on my suffering, for which you alone are to blame, writes Erika, immediately after the afternoon nap, my afternoon rest was ruined.

Prior to Erika going shopping in the afternoon, she writes, why are you so horrid to me, who loves you above all else and only you, Elsiebabefairy!

Karl is even feeling very peculiar! Very very peculiar. Isn't that then sufficient for proving my Love without ceasing?

How insatiable you are and destroy me without mercy. If you don't answer me straight away, I'll kill myself. You know precisely what a snake will do on my breast!, writes Erika when she's back from shopping.

At the end of the afternoon Erika writes, I've had enough. Give me the death-blow. I don't want to live any longer. The brutality of your heart stabs me maliciously and deceitfully. Only why?

How should I, writes Erika in the early evening, understand your barbaric destructive rage ... Oh I ..., writes Erika.

You?, writes Erika, *you do everything for me*, well how then? And when and where, Erika soon writes, after the evening has arrived. With this geranium morsing you can search the heavens, Elsiebabefairy. Over there you will find me again, you lousy lover who lets me travel ice cold into the tundra of insensitivity.

You cruel creature, writes Erika as soon as darkness is completely fallen, you beastly faithless Elseapparation, so that is how it is. So that is what you mean with your pretended Love that you dump me after everything! That you don't say anything more and let yourself be heard from after the many things that I have done for you. Did I not do everything for you!? More than everything!?

Do I not prove just now with the most dangerous thing that there is in the world, my Love!!?? Must I myself still fall on a dagger?? Which will then protrude from the tip of my breast with an ivory handle?? And my dearest Mother Mrs. Runk will cast herself inconsolably over me, who you have on your conscience!!?, writes Erika when the evening is coming to an end.

Whether I perish or not is all the same to you, writes Erika to Else before she goes to bed. You are a stone that no human being can move. It doesn't even affect its most fervent Lover, who can just die, extinguish and disappear. Who stones its One and Only with its silence, disembowels, you knacker!

I'm going to bed now and will cry until I die, to be miffed to death, to worry to death and to sleep to death. Tomorrow I will be no more. You alone are responsible for that, writes Erika before she gets into bed.

The night is here. It is fortunate that a night falls down from the heavens onto Erika who is finally asleep and writing no more letters.

17. THE DOCTOR

Hans is living happily at home, where the table is laid. Hans goes happily to work, where the world offers itself to him. But where Hans now lives and goes, he grows a little weaker. Hans always feels rather ill. Hans feels so ill. Even worse. Hans does not go to work any longer. Hans grows weaker and weaker. The Doctor says, Hans is sick. Hans cannot work. He does not know why Hans does not get well, says the Doctor. Hans Rinx has a weak constitution, says the Doctor, although one does not think that and does not see it. Now one sees it. Even though it is totally inexplicable. It will surely turn out alright, says the Doctor. Just do not lose courage, says the Doctor to Hans. Hans, of course, has a good Wife, who nurses him well. Better than that a man, who is ailing, cannot have, says the Doctor. Mrs. Else, says the Doctor, is an angel, how she nurses her sick Spouse Hans Rinx. Full of courage, says the Doctor. Rage, a Word rings in Hans's ears. It is so piercing and sharp and stabs him in the colon. Hans knows this Word of course. He is afraid. Mrs. Else is sacrificing herself for her Spouse, says the Doctor. Plucks out collars, Hans hears a strange male voice say. Hans gags in the throat on an enemy voice that pulls him on his collar. He is worried. And the gentleman in delirium has a good Mother for support, says the Doctor. Bite, whispers a voice the ear of Hans, good rest. Sharp Teeth bite into the liver of Hans. And in the small intestine whole multitudes of rats are gnawing. Rage and tranquillity? Oven glow? Which route are these serrated sets of teeth taking? Burn down everything. What kind of whispering about Hans goes on round him. Hey! shouts a voice. Hothey. Grave and peace and quiet, there is murmuring in the ear of Hans, under elms a scourge pauses and bleeds. Ooohaah, screams Hans. Just have a good rest, says the Doctor. Do not worry, says the Doctor. Such a stomach upset does pass. Your good Wife will cook a nice little soup for you which is strengthening. Your good Mother will fan a little breeze for you which cools. Ooooheeah!! screams Hans. Just do not get upset, says the Doctor. Here is a remedy says the Doctor, for your seriously ill Spouse. It will certainly show how effective it is, says the Doctor, you will see. Aaaaaoooh!!! screams Hans. Aaaahaaahaaaooooh!!! In his intestines a crocodile is feasting. Many crocodiles join in. Now don't act out, says the Doctor to the sick Hans. With your Angel Wife, says the Doctor, and with your Madonna Mother, he says, you are favoured by fortune. A little perspiring, says the Doctor, and it will all be over. *That* current Hans hears thundering through his conductors. The lightening flashes jab into Hans. There is a jerking in him and tearing and kindling. No, inflame on and on. And a hundred snares tauten the short circuit. And grave diggers speak of infiltration. They want to put an entirely alive Hans into a ground. They want to patch him without a lining and leave him dangling. Spike him with chestnuts when it's all over, Hans hears the adversary in his ear. There! a glacier slaps onto his forehead and cheeks. There! his calves are sticking in new snow. Change frequently, says the Doctor to Else. When the fever subsides, your spouse will be out of the woods.

Chapter Three

1.   A BREAK DOWN

Oh how tranquil is the world around Else all at once. Tactfully life keeps silence with regard to Else. Everywhere it is quiet and flat. Nowhere does a Word hail in on Else. Next door Hans is lying and rising painfully high. Erika shoves her piles of letters in at the door. Mother Rinx stacks her Mother Love in high story level layers at the bed of Hans. All around Else the world waves up in undulation. Hill and dale. Hill and dale. When the mountains collide with one another, it is impermeable. *Elsechickgorgeousyou.* When the valleys yawn apart, there is no place to hide. *Elsiebabefairy mine for always.* And with a deep décolleté a mother-in-law Rinx hikes through the mountains. Else sees the wide panorama. On the plan Else is hanging like a bush. Has no part. Does not impart. Files away at a joyful Future. *Elsechickgorgeousyou.* Everything else needs to be simply ground down. Planed off, harrowed, chipped. And afterwards grouted sealed and varnished. No hair crack is allowed to exist after that. Muteness must be. Modest but mine, cannot be sung out of Else today because of the silence. In the valleys the sidesteps takes from her fate echo. Where the World bows to itself. Dents itself. From Erika the bitch she bolts away. If only Erika does not hear the noise! If only Erika does not see the glacier tongue licking away into the plain! The icy freezing must not be noticed by any Erika. Else withdraws into a holding place of peace. Into the lead-grey small kitchen fume extractor hood. There is a little corner free for Else. Mother Rinx climbs through the tangled sleep of her son. She will hike through and burrow herself in again. In she will climb and rest in the chimnies of his inordinate desires. He must shout. Be obliged to howl the mind out of his body. The intercourse. Something will remain. That will be assigned to Mrs. Rinx. It belongs to Mrs. Rinx and to Mrs. Rinx alone. In there Mother Rinx will direct. For the remainder of all life. There will be no giving out. Else will be eliminated from the family circular railway. Hans will be locked out from having anything to say. Worry? Mother Rinx will rummage in the profusion of her desires. She will organise a desire shower. Beneath the desire drizzle she will bloom and thrill. In the screaming landscape of her good son Mrs. Rinx reclines and waits. Lies in wait for all desirable promises. At the porthole where life slips in and out. Hans sleeps an exhausted sleep. Mother Rinx keeps watch over the good Hans. He must not want to bolt. He is deeply in debt to his good mother. *Elsiebabefairy beloved sunshine even if you push me into the abyss that is deeper than every bottomless pit, I love you and cry my eyes out of the sockets of my skull and my Mother Runk is wringing her hands over her head over my terrible condition on account of your ruthless behaviour.* The gorges drop off uncannily quietly. Else is on top. Else looks down. At a distance the land lies soundlessly beneath Else. Does not stir so that Else does not take fright. That Else feels how a wave of tranquility rocks Else. However Else moves and acts, what she does not do, the chasms rest discreetly. *Elsechickgorgeousyou you are like a colibri that I saw in the zoo. Each feather is of a different colour, not merely like a peacock that has different colours, but the same on each feather. You are something special to me, Elsechickgorgeousyou each separate feather specially bright.* A cheerful fragrance wafts up out of some or other Past. A colourful image lights up out of some or other memory residue. Here in the kitchen Else dances in a real Present Time with HansTheGlance. Beneath gay Now maypole ribbons Hans is a Poet in Else. Beneath a velvet blue Now night sky HansTheGlance says the most beautiful real Words. *Elsechickgorgeousyou your gaze is a promise until death when I look at you*, Else hears the ear creator Hans say accompanied by his moans and groans and screaming. Now two simultaneous times collide in the repose of Else's condition. In the fanfares of a brass band music a pitiful Hans sound explodes. Without making a noise themselves, two tones meet one another. They are the hooks of two times that would like to meet each other. They are a nail which hits onto the head of Else. In the Else brain box they separate. Else cannot tell them apart. Like the sharp iron entering into the blood stream or membranes or something like that. Misses. Does not cut. Is at the same time the forehead of Else. Is a sharp soft metal. Is a grey compact mass the red sea. Everything cohabits in Else's head. *Elsechickgorgeousyou you are like an innocent white sheet of paper, on which I am the Word. You are all around me in complete purity.* Is a red even swell. A watch-tower? No-one in it is worn out. No Erika is buried in it. Erika wants to particularly stay stuck in the rusty swamp. Reddens herself in a scree in which she discovers Else. No bush on a plain into which Else transfigures herself. Does not burn. Does not burn. Dead quiet all around the crevices sag. What kind of peace stares around Else. How gentle and slender Hans lies in the rocks and moans. Thanks Else with his screams. With howling and bawling Hans bows before his Spouse. The loud laments of Hans seep away in the garbage. Up above Else impatiently looks forward to the echo. There is none in the dense peaks of the world. Else does not hear one. Else is swooning in the Waves. Hill. Dale. Hill. Mrs. Rinx wears snake skin on her feet. The mountain range is merciful. Why? Mother Rinx bears her blonde waved head though the mountains. Her heels clatter in the rock. The late departed Mr. Rinx hears every desire of his Spouse. She hammers each one onto the stone of her path. He must now become aware of each one in his grave, the late departed Mr. Rinx. He must hear that she is making claims on his flesh. Step by step each one jars shrilly at the threshold of Hans. Hans must not try to roll away. How he rumbles on his bed. He will have to fortify himself for the nature of nature. *Elsechickgorgeousyou*! On this hillock Else is alone with her Husband HansIloveyou. On this hill Else is alone with her Wedded Thought HansIloveyou. How a breeze rises freely into the heavens! How a draught of breath ascends into the bluish firmament. Shimmers here velvet in the gentleness milky and tender. Far! Larger and bright and open HansIloveyou extends over Else. Hollows out *Elsechickcolibri! Elsechickseablue*!! Else's Spouse excavates from out of a neighbouring room. Out from a construction site with admission denied. Else simply pricks her ears. So beautiful. *Elsechickpureareyoudevourme*! Else knows it is right. Else is white and pure and gobbles up every Word. Else remains unsullied. She grows on the stilts of the Words. HansIloveyou waits behind a veil and dawdles. Grouses. Says get married. Here a small sign moves itself. Bursts out and babbles get married. *Then we will both be married forever, Elsiebabefairy. Then we will be independent. Then there will only still be us two in the world. Unceasingly only you and me, Elsiebabefairy pretty ringlet. And our Mother Runk of course, who untiringly looks after us*. Erika stands out in the flat fields. From out of the depressions with no hiding place. Where incidents lurk in a mist, the bother Erika taunts. Else is an unpacked concern in this mouth delta. An Erika transaction boils up the unsecured terrain. An Erika event springs out here and there from the surroundings. An Erika untoward occurrence splashes between all public papers. A scene rushing in the wide fanned out Erika is taking aim at Else. Else does not know every open pore! Where Erika is able to get into Else everywhere! With a letter Erika strolls into the carapace Else. Flares around in Else with every arbitrary Word. Drives Else around on a battue. Arrests Else on a comma. Which never comes to rest in Else. Lacerates around in Else. Everyone tramples around at will in Else. As a situation demands. Not Else. Else twinkles a little song up on the hillock. Does not come out from Else. It is so tranquil up here. Else bleats the Ballad of Freedom up here on the hump. Not heard by anyone. There is such a thick cotton wool of air. Else cranks out her Hymn of Hymns of Hymn of Hearken in complete silence! Listen! HansIloveyou is the only good Husband up here where Else nurses him. The good HansIloveyou revives himself with Else who feeds him. A good

Wife belongs to a HansTheGlance. Now he is nourished by the good Else. As the good Father says. A little here a little there, like this a good Else coddles her HansIloveyou. This is how the Else mutes her good Wedded Husband. At last a good Else can do something good for a good Husband. As bidden by the good Father. Must by all means graze a little, the good Husband. Pasture a little in the good bitter pasture-land. Browse a little in the good corroding water-meadow. The good Else will feed the HansIloveyou. As the good fellow needs. So that the good Father is in the right. As always. *An innocent sheet of white paper on which I am the Word.* As before in the early summer. When the summer was endless in complete correctness. When it was summer from early to late. When the dance carried on beneath the gay ribbons. On. When the night sky was velvet. And Else a great black velvet that covers everything. A sponge that absorbs everything. Every Word that Hans is. Every sentence out of which Hans makes a world that has value. Every book that a written off Hans is. A ready-made Hans in a ready-made world. Hangs an Else onto it, the appendix. An Else straddling a good beginning and a permanent culminating point. Now. Where no stake drives in that interrupts everything. Which simply makes a dot in all oration. In an endangered Else existence, done and dusted. No more digging up and smoothing over. In the midst of an entire literary character where no good Husband makes a hot air display? Else is a successful hutch fit in a marriage landscape. Vibrates up above in the well-known tranquility. Buzzes. Hans is supposed to make a Word. *Elseclauseareyoumyword.* No Words no Voice no Tones for Talking for Singing does a Hans utter. Does not imagine any Else. Leaves the poor reality whirring around in a world. Giving himself alone a Name in the empty spaces. Kicks about a little. No bamboozling. No deception. Only a complaining grunting and groaning. Alternating sodium and manganese and cobalt and vanadium. But no Good Night Kiss. There is a dreadful drought up here on the mountains where Else so gladly survives a good night with her good Husband. There is such a tangled tranquility. That is able to really agitate an Else. So far has an Else come in the literal arms of her good HansTheGlance. His fleshly fingers rot off from him. Together with an unspeakable body. How Else has a terrible sympathy with her good Father. Good Husband! Else does not know exactly. Did Hans say heaven? Heaven, says the dear good Hans and spreads himself far and bright blue from star to star. *Elsechickextracolourfulyou are a colibri that has another colour on every feather, so beautiful and splendid!* Dark blue? A mother-in-law pokes a blonde waved head into the night sky. But here a mother-in-law has gone astray. Has lost her way beneath the nocturnal maypole ribbons. Here is a brass band that grows horns. Here is a Hans Rinx the Poet, too with the magic spells. Smells of blooming lime-trees. A summer. Smells of fresh evening. A summery HansTheGlance. But here is no Mother Rinx! Hans Rinx would definitely have told an Else that. Tommmmtrrralaaah! says the brass band. For sure. *Gorgeousareyouelsemyclause*, says Hans Rinx. That is all that Hans Rinx says. Groans a little at the same time and howls. And after all the continual groaning the Wedded Husband still has to vomit. Like a heron, says the good Father. Just fly at last, Hans, says Else to her Husband. Spread out your heron wings, says Else. Grey-white stuff is vomited by the free- as – a bird Hans. Get your wings in a row and and set spurs to the spores, says Else to her Spouse. In such a high flight the worlds reverse their routes rods. Powers. The pilots make haste with a strainer. Being. The Word shunting railway yard Rinx Hans granulates the stinking horror out from a mouth piece. *Mamma*, murmurs Hans, *Elseclausegorgeousyou are my physician in suffering and sorrow.* A whispering rises up the mountain to Else. *Mammahelp!* up here in the rarified air an Else hears her good HansTheGlance whisper out from the ether. Oh, *that* Mamma is who the good Hans means. Let her help him then. If she can. Cans full of mercy and goodness and auxilliary temporal Words. Understood. Does not hurt anyone.

A wind blows uniformly from only one totally unified direction. From Erika to Hans and to Mother Rinx over to Else. Sweeps over the close mountains full of affliction agreement. Indulgent Hans stretches over all that geodectically. Full of pathways into the heavens and back is the good Idea Hans. *Darling think again of the lovely chain swinger with which we fly into the sky only we two together in the breezes* and so on Erika burrows herself into the joint while brooding where the prose drains a terrain. Jerks a bit. So that there is more room. Crashing with her purse or box or something. Is very joyful. Is in the hands of a share company. Worships her wether Karl to the skies. Else cooks for her Spouse Hans. Stays and feels the same style. Darns these flocks for him. Listen! At home a skinny girl arouses interest. Is conscious of a pick-up line. Sends a little hurdle toward a Husband. Whore! *Miiiiddniiiightt??* Gives a Mrs. Rinx the damage report. For her stupid skull. Stupid blonde crown, above. Sob throat. The insurance has to cough up. Else can hear it in the low land. First the trains rumble. There is quite a lot of thundering coming from the plain. A noise is not able to hide away anywhere in these event drifts. Wells up to Else into the square. Splashes down without an echo. Here it is quiet? Here the silence cannot be broken. It is so silent. The contortions congeal into resin. Do not come up at all. The sins grow fainter and fainter. Choke. Mull a sensation. To limit a screw thread. Breaks. Vomits out every custom. Concession. Becomes totally used to vomiting. Turning pale. The paunch stares shockingly out from its wound. From its spout. Stop it! Hans is not supposed to clear out everything from this violin case. Otherwise there will be no Hans left over for the bright side of things. For fiddling. Else sees a light illuminating this tunnel of song. Else hears bright rays land on this drum of blue. Here Else devises a ford. Searches for a square. Quick. Quick! What a distance! Designation. Step by step out into the ground work. Past the Dogs-past Sirius. Stars. Stars? Brows. A blue flickers a head light flares up and extinguishes, flares up and exits *into the sky we will fly again only us two together into the air* ...

2.   THE SUICIDE. THE WINGS.

Else comes to her senses. Where did an Else travel to on her thought travel vehicle, a head that does not explode into pieces?

Is the slut beside herself? Why doesn't the beast just die? Rip the bandage off the whore! Poke the wretched bitch! Hit the guts! Give her a good drubbing the whore!!! Get off the old tomboy, the dumbledore with the jumbled excuse. Throttle the dumbledore!

A world in forty versions tugs at Else. Tears at her bandage. At her hair. Piercing Word Missiles penetrate Else. Shake at the foundations of her security. What sort of a rabble is that? Where are the walls? Where is the skin? Where is the good Wedded Husband Hans building his heaven? Pitching his patch?

Slowly Else punctures the artery with the prong of the fork. Else methodically bores and channels the terrain. There is no pain the blunt fork with its prongs. It wants to evade the entire skin everywhere. Evade, not burst. Else dashes her wrist onto the fork. The prongs do not want to drill into the sinews or what? No real blood flow spurts out. Is hurting horribly now. But to no purpose. The human being just does not want to give way out of Else. Not a soul or something like that. Not a thought steps away from the brooding. Is so senseless, the zinc cutlery in a prison. Does not make sense. Scratch the eyes out of this cockroach! Flay her the tight frock the feeler this fumbling. Slit the throat of the rat the jaw! Take her out by the scruff of her neck into the cupboard so that she is scared. Suffocates. She must devour her own Narcissus the cunt. Murderess! Rattle in the throat until she is stoned. Cleansed. Chop the thighs into little rissoles! Entice the hen into the pond! Lard the soft parts with spatulas. With stocking sticks. Roast the little rose over the candle. From the heart.

Ahhhh! screams Else. Aaaahhhh!!! Help! Help! Help! A wardress comes running. She pulls Else out of forty synonyms of pain. A Supervisor drags Else out from forty hate attributes into a single cell. Out from forty loathing attacks. Out from episodes of mortal terror. An Else cannot be kept in a sick-bay. In the medical centre Else is a doomed woman for sure.

Head off. Corrugate the skirt. Rrrrip! Brew and demolish this skirt chassis! Club! Throttle the carousing seed the woman! The Garden of Eden honey tart! Flay the flesh into a three cart-load Word the ice cold crone! Weld shut.

Else has cold sweat on the Brow. Else has a thousand lances in an Ear. Drive terribly into the Abdomen so that it cringes. Labour pains eh eeehh pinches. Else is one single lump of misery. Her left Arm bears a big white bandage. Ridiculous! Else tears it off. Only the Sinews are damaged. Only the Wrist is swollen thick. A little tetanus. The Artery throbs restlessly and irregularly. Does not permit itself to be detoured by a soft zinc fork. Does not permit itself to simply bleed out! A terrible lot of blood that must come out of Else squirts around in a Body. With all the liquid a HansIloveyou can cleanly splash out of Else. Can click an Erika along in a red stream. Can ooze a stinking mean trick of the world out from Else. In the end Else is a Nice Daughter again. In the end a good Father takes pleasure in a good daughter Else. She has greatly disappointed him, his Else. A good Father works unceasingly with a slate stylus on a familial ideal calligraphy that only a Father devises, he means it so well. Drives dreadful thunderbolts back into the Word prison, a really well-intentioned Father! Leads past something of the Past. Beats a forgetting out from the good hiding places. Death – halloo!!, shouts the Father, Death-halloo!

Screams along, the time that does not elapse. Recur, the shrieks the mummy of doing and talking. Shining and in cash retribution is extracted coin by coin, tit for tat. Lying fallow in a Head of Else who wants to rest on the slat-bed, the capital. Else wants to be void. Wants to be docile and dead and tired. Wants to lie down and stare out of the cell window into the night. Waiting for a sleep to come a death. Now a sky over a prison perforates a black hole. The spitting sparks of a memory spray white onto a Scalp of Else. Break through! Inflame great giant-size images of horror. Stare from a sky into a dark rock-bottom. A great black grave is the hole that in the cell is a window. Both square flags wave precisely over one another. The flags change from black to ink blue. The surfaces are dipped in something. The surroundings beam yellow red white the cold powerlessness. A black coffin plunges into this long, long sea blue. It is so pitiless there outside. There is screaming. Spray whips rather high and breaks. It stinks. The decay stinks dreadfully. Shovel it in! Shovel it in! What is going on inside there no human being is permitted to know. Especially an Else Rinx not at all! A slimy liquid is circulating in her. Clogs the pores for thinking. But in no way goes out from Else. An abominable trap is a Skin all around a Body. A strict penal colony is fenced in, in such a stuffed-out Skin. A crude natural force raves in the Torso and Limbs and Head and Foot of Else. In a thousand pieces. A rather considerable horror is in Else's material stocks. Else knows precisely. Blood squirts through and through in Else's wretched Body. White and fluid, it thickens in the sack. A hammering Pulse hastens around between Neck and Hand and Sole. A Breath stiffens from out of a Throat. It just does not want to travel though the Lungs. Just breathe Hans! Breathe! You have to draw breath. Do listen Hans! Spread the sails the wings wide for the breeze HansIloveyou. For the radiant rigid journey that an Else Rinx pays for her Spouse.

Do not scream Hans.

It is raining so much. The maypole ribbons made of crépe paper become soggy. The gay colour runs out from the colourful happiness. Money in the afternoon and children in the morning rain down on the bridal couple.

Do not scream Hans it is nothing.

The Light Eternal is shining on someone, says the Priest. The Priest walks to an open pit. Mounds of earth heaped up all around. Pall bearers wait with a coffin. Is somebody inside. They wear black robes. Bear dark red noses. The last dignified flag is fluttering for somebody on his final day of celebration. Somebody is lying so small and so pale inside the package. Somebody is lying so powerlessly shut in this wooden box. A Mother Rinx old as the hills stands at a grave and folds her hands.

Do not scream Hans it cannot be that bad. Drink the chamomile. It helps you to be calm.

A Light Eternal shines into an arid hollow Mother grave shines eternally into a has-been diva brush almost without bristles into a desert honeysuckle a bare Mother sickle stabs eternally the derision of the sour strong-box the deaf spinet sunken Mother tunnel. Not a single thunderbolt impedes the impetus of these stream rapids. Their under currents.

Do not scream Hans. Screaming does not help. Your blonde waved Mother Rinx opens her heart to you after everything. Flies toward you. Constructs crutches for you. Both Rinx women Sr. and Jr. stand by your side. Erika pokes her head in at the door. Convinces herself of the progress. The good Mother Mrs. Runk comes with the Doctor. The Doctor does not understand Hans Rinx. How Mr. Rinx is always screaming and whimpering! Never has anybody been better cared for than the sick Mr. Rinx. How Mr. Rinx wails and rattles in the throat! He must not malinger if he pleases, the young Mr. Rinx. So young and such hypersensitive behaviour! Every day at midday and in the evening beef-tea with an egg. That strengthens the constitution, Mr. Rinx. And continue with compresses on the calf against the fever, good Wife you Angel. And cold poultices on the forehead, good Mother Madonna. Do not snivel, Mr. Rinx. That does not become you. In two or three days the Doctor will call again, says the Doctor. Then things will be decidedly better, says the Doctor, if not good. Let us pull ourselves together a little, Mr. Hans Rinx. Otherwise only the hospital remains that helps, good women, says the Doctor, that would surely make the good women feel sorry, says the Doctor.

3.   THE MISFORTUNE

A blonde waved Mother Rinx picks up a scent. Here something is smelling off. Here a use by date has expired. Here the everlasting loser Mrs. Rinx must once again leave empty-handed. Mother Rinx sits down on the kitchen chair and ruminates. A wall clock ticks and ticks so that Mrs. Rinx will soon go crazy. The son is somehow oozing away. To somewhere his colour his flesh his breath his motivation. Without putting up a fight he allows himself to be eaten away by an illness. Without revolt he allows himself to be consumed by something dubious. Has become such a shadow. Is no longer an echo of a sound. Silences himself somehow out of the world. A Mother Rinx cannot get her head around that. There will be a misfortune if something does not happen. Something must happen immediately. Otherwise something dreadful will come to pass. Here a baby is being thrown out with the bath water. An impalpable destiny is brewing. A taciturn Wailing Wall Hans Rinx is shielding something terribly reprehensible by his Wedded Wife Else. Has something to do with women's bodies. Uniting themselves against a Mother Rinx who they force out of an alliance. Unfurle from their buxom luscious flesh venereal thighs posterior fingertips alabaster milk breasts a body chain that will throttle a poor Hans Rinx. Strangle somehow. Is already almost not able to criticize, this lamentable scrawny Hans. Emits so much air and fluid. Is not able to keep anything down the cataleptic idyll Hans. Does not heed any call of the blood by his Mamma the poor poor Hans. Does not endure his Mother Rinx any more, who has a vested right in natural law! Mother Rinx sits on the kitchen chair and taps on the floor with the heel of her shoe. Here Mrs. Rinx must thoroughly deliberate on it. A horizon is falling off a heaven a body a bodily Son. Does a complete Mrs. Rinx world disappear just like that? A monotonous honest Mrs. Rinx life without a trace? Without a gratitude that once beat a thunder on a drum! Without a remembering everything wants to blur! Does a desire of a Mother Rinx never bloom up into an enormous white peony! Does a wound of a Mother Rinx never blanch to a grief. Is a dignity creeping secretly away from a place of waiting. And an eternally stupid Mother Rinx is again sitting here unassuming and invisible. Left to be a wallflower. Left in the lurch by a class lottery that is not drawn. No Word is supposed to remain for a Mrs. Rinx no flesh no sex no entitlement. Simply slips by just like that before her eyes Hans her only body. Her necessitous consumption. Hans shrinks away beneath her fingers. The robust muscle son with the glowing red cheeks fades away. There a clock is ticking a lapse. In this snug realm a family easily takes a seat, of course. Mother Rinx sits on the kitchen chair and contemplates. Cuckoo! Cuckoocuckcoo!! Half past one already! Something has to happen soon. Immediately! Mother Rinx sees a geranium at the kitchen window. Oh this eternally cantankerous monstrous plant. She will presently hurl it onto the street in a high curve the peculiar thing. Mother Rinx plucks around her blonde waved hair with her fingers. Adjusts it. Order has to start internally in a life and extend outwardly. Mother Rinx opens the window and throws the flowering pot plant out of her existence in a grand trajectory. It had obstructed something essential. That is soon seen by Mother Rinx.

4. INTERNAL NAVIGATION

Oh, says Mrs. Runk, good child, be sensible. Think of Else your dearest friend good child.

Oh, says Erika, but I'm thinking of nothing other than of Elsiebabefairy my other worldly life my heavenly power.

For two days Karl Runk moans in his bed. Yes. Karl Runk. He is suddenly living by the side of his Wedded Wife. That is unusual. Mr. Runk does not get up. Mr. Runk does not go away. Karl Runk is a Married Man who knows at last for what purpose he has acquired a Wife. Erika plucks at the sheet. Erika plumps the pillow. Erika pulls the feather bed straight. Feeds the Mr. Runk with fennel tea. Erika is performing a Labour of Love for her Husband. Karl Runk puffs himself up inexplicably to the Wife.

Oh, says Erika venomously, he is my proof of a Husband. When he is there, here with us. Otherwise the neighbours say, Erika does not really have a Wedded Husband. Who keeps her in line or dips and dabs. The Mr. Runk takes flight. Mr. Karl Runk operates at a distance, the neighbours like saying.

Mr. Karl Runk fluffs up his feathers a little at home in his own stable. That is normal for a recumbent Married Man. Mr. Runk likes to show off a bit in front of his Wedded Wife when he stays. Mr. Karl Runk is a special resident stag when he arrives. Karl Runk prepares himself in the nuptual bed. Feels poorly today. Very poorly.

Oh says Erika venomously, how good it is when a Wedded Husband comes. When her Karl Runk gladly drinks his fennel tea from the hand of his Wife. Here a little there a little. When her Marital Status

Karl does not hearken any hunting call from the world which is so turbulent. Karl is catapulted far away from his Marriage. Finds a track back to Erika Runk with difficulty. Shows himself so seldom at the house door of the Bond for Life. Erika shows her Wedded Husband Karl a great act of loving kindness. He feels poorly today, very poorly.

Mr. Runk is a stallion. Today he gets into a gallop with a little difficulty. Seethes too much. Today Karl is pleased to be in the proximity of his Spouse. Something always helps. Here a little there a little. Something easily causes the winds to abate. Today or tomorrow something thaws in the fleeting imaginary Husband. Conjures up for him a sort of pink garland or something like that. A sort of echo of a bugle call kill wedding march or something like that. Pity that he feels so poorly.

Oh says Erika venomously, how gladly an Erika lets all sorts of things drop. A Mr. Karl Runk is a platitude in the life of each and every woman. Karl can be such a rich internal navigation. Never should the Husband have departed from the marriage harbour. All piers and the whole thingamy there is decaying. In the entire neighbourhood Erika is a laughing-stock. Mr. Runk as Wedded Husband lets himself be seen so seldom after all. Today he is staying here, the Mr. Runk. He is feeling so poorly today.

Actually the Wedded Husband Karl Runk is in a bit of a hurry. Outside in the whole city something is waiting for him. Sooner or later a tartan pleated skirt is longing. Today or tomorrow a pleated skirt will be looking for him. Friday. Today! Poor Mr. Runk is lying in the bed of his Spouse. Ruining amusing human contacts. Karl Runk wants to quickly get out of bed. Cannot lift up his excessively fermenting torso. Have to go! Have to go! A Mr. Karl Runk lies reluctantly fallow. Mr. Runk is feeling poorly of course.

Oh, says Erika resentfully, Mr. Runk is not supposed to say that. To have to go away. In the end it could be very far away.

Oh, flutters Mrs. Runk energetically, that is enough child.

Well, soothes Erika. It's all a poisonous joke. One doesn't have to take it seriously. It's a nice toxic warning so that the Husband doesn't stray too far. Elsiebabefairy rose mound can understand how Love binds.

Well, says Mrs. Runk, send him away your Husband. He must go. Quickly! Your good Mother is staying forever. Your good Mother is here for you. In difficulty and danger your little loose screw breaks very easily. Your Karl Runk must hop it quickly. Depends too much on his leg carrying no weight.

Go, says Erika. Quickly Karl go!

5.   THE CASKET

A brisk breeze is shooting through. Howling a little between the cemetery markers. A few figures in black clothing are standing at a grave. Lose themselves in threads of discourse crosses. Else is standing at an open pit and is looking down. There is a casket down there. Yes. There is a simple pine wood coffin down there. There somebody is ending his life in a very modest box. In between the tranquil trees somebody is coming to rest. Quite calmly a little breeze strews dust around the yew hedges. A Priest is standing at the place and speaking. Somebody has departed from us, says the Priest. Somebody has left us after a long and difficult illness, says the solemn Priest. Has lost someone's poor brother, the poor poor Priest. A granite old Mother Rinx in a black coat stands next to the Grave. Is as quiet as a piece of granite. Stands at a hole like a grave stone. The Light Eternal is shining on somebody, the poor Priest shoots between the grave markers. What is an Else doing here, wonders an Else Rinx. A finger of light travels down from the cloud. Jabs into the pine graining. Is somebody hermetically nailed in down the in the Lap of Abraham. Mother Rinx wrings slate-grey fingers. There! Erika is at the funeral, too. Wearing a black mourning band on a grey coat. Casts her eyes down the rascal. Antennaextentioniceball. Auroradestructiveairplane. Cockand bullhomejourneyproduct. Curfewgateentrance, attempts Else. Erika does not smile. Erika does not even look over at Else. Holds fast onto the jacket sleeve of Mother Runk. Does Erika not find a tickle nice today? Can usually not get enough. Has a steep frown between the eyes. Has sweat droplets on a forehead and nose. Hans is a little blueish in the face. Or is it green? Puffs a little or blows. Has no tone in any muscle. Does not make any sound. Constricts his soul his throat the poor poor Hans. Erika bends over the lump of human being in the bed. The face of an Erika shines Eternal Light. May Light Eternal shine on somebody whispers the Priest. A sun rises for Erika as never before. Shines and shines and shines. Somebody is going home. Anchors a marker in the yew forest. A light wind howls an arrow. May someone be merciful to his lost soul, rasps the Priest. Amen, responds a marble grey Mother Rinx in a black coat. Who is playing such a curious game here? Else knows no rules. Does not make any correct move. No children. No prospects. Internally in Else something is fresh and bloody. Internally in Else a mother bubble fills itself taut and bursts. Flows in rills a blood down the legs from out of a dry well. A pregnant orifice opens the gate to output. An Else just now fervently loves her down fallen HansTheGlance, who today and here is so very absent. Where is he? Everything is desolate here without him. All are benumbed the figures the black gills. A hurricane is approaching. The leaves on the treetops are a little giddy. Trumpet blooms of revenge! Arrivaldrydustabsurdity! Moneygamegrassconcaveseal! Alarmbuttonsireninsurance! Algaedrawingstrawstalkinvestment! There is no getting though to Erika today. HansTheGood does not utter a Poet's Word from behind the hidden curtain either. There is no making sense of the world at all on such a day. Here nobody can tell Else something. That is a day with nothing more than fractured world parts. A coherence is lacking. Else knows that precisely. There an Else cannot allow herself to be irritated. Will go crazy otherwise. Everything and everyone all around Else is gravitating somewhere else. Else is stuck in the middle and will cut herself into little pieces? An Else makes a mess bit by bit of a day that is no good. That does not rain, that does not speak, that does not count. A summing up that someone is playing here piece by piece scatters for Else. The cutout fortunately has a firm frame. Does not abruptly change the scene in the middle of its place. Turns over the pages page by page from the same cut.

6.   THE SIREN'S VOICE

The Light Eternal may shine on somebody.

Yes, says Else.

Keeps on shining in the darkness.

Yes, says Else.

He is pleased to keep on phosphorescing in the shade.

Yes, says Else to the Voice that is speaking.

The hair keeps on shining so beautifully and shimmers.

Yes, says Else.

The eyes keep on sparkling vivaciously and lovingly.

Yes, says Else. It is like that.

Their vivacious flickering keeps on leading a weak flesh into temptation.

Yes, says Else.

The splendid green keeps on burning magnificently in porous grounds.

Yes, says Else.

The white innocent doom keeps on burning a little in the stomach.

Yes, says Else.

Burst magnificently easily the splendid green pustules.

Yes.

Vomit so easily the green gall the antimony angels.

Yes.

Shimmer in the darkness when a pulse races and hammers and gallops.

Yes.

Her skin is a hot and dry mirror a lightish one.

--

They shiver glowing white in the bat of an eyelid the smoke eliminator, says a Voice that Else knows.

--

They jerk in convulsive dream vices. Chirrup in a terribly echoless forest, says a Voice.

Yes, Yesyesyes! shouts Else.

Misfortune is a terrible poison in the world, says Erika.

Yes, says Else.

A poisoned arrow is a misfortune, so rapidly does it hit into a defective control room, says Erika.

Yes, says Else.

A tiny pinch of misfortune daily is sufficient, says Erika.

Yes, says Else.

Just a very minute grain of misfortune is able to completely poison a life, says Erika.

Yesyes, says Else. Does not have a clue what she is talking about, an Erika with her tomfoolery of a piece of poetry in her head which she pours into letters just like that.

Piles itself up and up and becomes a hill, a mountain a rocky abyss, whispers Erika.

Does not know what a Past can comprise, such a shrewdly chattering along Erika Runk so that an Else loses her temper her head.

Nobody crosses over from the deep gorges only the Voice of the Siren. Sounds sweet and complains and clings, grinds emery Erika.

Will soon trumpet out everything an Else Rinx ignite all fanfares. All the monsters that are blown up behind the peep-show in looking back at what has been.

Nothing can be such a toxic poison, chirps Erika like an bewitching sound. Swings in a body.

What then does an Erika Runk, who crouches life-long behind a mother smock, believe! First a Mother labours out a Child. Once the work is done, such a Woman is no good for anything anymore. Not for satisfaction. Seduction. But nature does not have this in mind for a former Mother.

Tickles and whips, nuzzles Erika, and raves and charms and rubs and is greedy for and scatters and tautens a drum the banging Voice.

Was not envisaged by the mother-in-law that she would let her son knock her up. Had naturally long ago expired, the vexing question. The mutual draft was completely covered. Nobody needs to know.

Sparkles from blinding! Erika's Voice shakes a little.

Everything dried up forever. Thanks to mother nature. Available for re-use. Looked at this way garbage in any case. Help yourself gratis for recyclers!

A distinct sham screen of arsenic for the vermin! Blot the scoundrels out! says a shaking Erika Voice.

Some sort of homemade underhand insane sense allows this bill of exchange to be discovered. Lets an unfathomably mean trick come to light for an Else. A Mother-in-law is knitting little romper pants. Before Else's eyes a mockery puffs up a Homeric laugh.

Such a very tiny bit of misfortune can be a fatal poison in the course of a life, remarks an eternally unsuspecting Erika.

Before Else's face a chalk white father Hans Rinx whimpers and whines, who gets away once more. Little foetus departs after four months. Secretly into the city sewage. Home.

Can so very little destruction be so malignant aaas to devastate a family tableau, bleats Erika.

Does not suspect a jot of a mother-in-law, who calls out for pest control. Damage control. Get up! Else. Get up! Nobody hears something like that more distinctly in the ear than an Else who feels it in every bone. What sort of a clueless ninny is an Erika who belongs to a mother her whole life long! Who hangs onto Mamma's coat tails and would like to play a little destiny so that she has one, too. Literally. Erika in her little alphabetical goosey daisies, the poor goose, forges a little wreath on Else's wrist. Wears her splendidly beautiful jacket with the magnificent tambour embroidery work this divine grace in a world full of perplexities and ugliness.

Has such a pretty green tinge the frightening misfortune, says a Voice.

Yes, says Else. It is a simple as that.

Has eight nice triangles on the outside the arsenical acid, says a Voice. Blooms in five triangular surfaces a purgtory for a debtor. Incrusted in rhombic prisms. A clolour error inside a frantic fellow. Traveller.

Yes, says Else. Looks full of peace and innocent the white crystalline gem. The gentle eccentric goblin.

Dwells between phosphorous and antomonythe magnificent goody-two-shoes. Secretly hand to hand. Has everyone his fair chance in the competition of application. Alteration, says a Voice that Else knows. Converts itself by means of the smelting of arsenic gravel. By means of kisses of light steel green-coloured substitute matrixes in granular and stalked aggregates.

Yes, says Else. It is a gullible partner for life. Tidies up clean and orderly in the lead-grey house. Finally everything falls into place. Where it belongs. A profound silence comes into the ward where the entire Else is assembled. In case.

Death isn't the misfortune, says the self-willed stubborn Voice of Erika. It's the always waiting and waiting and waiting that has now come to an end Elseibabefairy. My blooming miracle here you have my silver thimble. It's dipped in my blood that belongs to you like my Future and Past bursting with the bliss of a sun-like Love into which we are now intertwined without end. Your Ek.

Never does an Erika comprehend anything. Everything remains sealed up. An Erika will never come to know. Never ever.

7.   THE WEDDED WIFE

Else Rinx visits her Husband in the hospital. For three long days for an hour in the mornings. In the afternoons half a one. The patient Hans Rinx is very weak. He needs rest. He is fed artificially. He is semi-conscious in utter agony. Her Spouse will soon die my good woman, says the Doctor. Just wring your hands good Mother Madonna, says the Doctor. Oh, says the Doctor, she is not here at all, the good Mother Madonna! Hans Rinx will pass away. You must be prepared for that. He is done for. Hans Rinx lies there, a sort of obstinate fore runner hand of a clock. It has quite certainly become too late. Quite certainly the agreement is expiring. Retches a little. Has not much more to retch. Has become such a filigree skeleton. The blood coagulates thickly in fat vein bulges on his hand. Does not want to go to the heart away from the heart. Else sees what Hans wants to say. *Elsechickgorgeousyou. Elsechickgorgeousyou like a colibri.* Hans Rinx is not able to speak any more. He moves his lips feebly. Else is reading. Else loves her Poet HansTheGlance. Hans Rinx loves his Else very much! He is leaving his tired body behind, which is really no good to an Else. He is leaving his atonement there for Else. He is leaving his horrid horribly good Mother here for Else as fodder. He goes on his way as a thought. Upward. Everything now belongs to Hans, which includes Else. His ardent Wife. Everything belongs to Hans that is in the air and on the earth. The maypole ribbons! Red! Green! Yellow! Blue! Limp and faded by the many winds. Sun and moon and stars are suspended in the world of Hans on a firmament arch. Velvet blue. Yellow lamp signalers. A polka. No. A gallop. The Words move along at a fox trot. When a Hans says a Word and the things move on from one state to the other. From the State of Marriage to the Widow's Weeds. Cinnamon pastry snails lay Words over the things rightly and wrongly. Cinnamon-coloured a first star rises up from a grey-blue twilight.

As Hans wishes. You have fulfilled all requirements. You have.

Hans Rinx dies quickly in the house of the sick. There is nothing left on him. Food Poisoning stands on the Death Certificate.

8.   THE FURNISHINGS

Erika Runk stands door frame under the wings of Mother Runk. Now she wants to be welcomed. Now she wants to harvest her fruits.

Elsiebabefairy angel you Eden on earth!

Please step aside, says Else. She is heaving the matress through the bedroom door.

But Elsiebabefairy you silver sweetness of my life's expectations, cheeps Erika.

Can you take a step back, says Else. I cannot get past. She pushes the matress onto the stair landing. Leans it against the door.

My dear daughter Erika will gladly help you at any time, Mrs. Runk assists her dear daughter Erika.

Else walks into the bedroom. Throws Hans's clothes into a large jute sack and ties it closed.

But Elsiebabefairy.

Else drags the jute sack to the front of the door. It is now the matresses neighbour. In the bedroom Else puts the handkerchief the comb the water glass the cotton wool ear plugs the dummy the Vaseline and all the bits and pieces into a shoe box. Else closes it with a rubber band. She opens the door to the Cabinet of the mother-in-law and tosses the box inside.

Else my child do speak with my dear daughter Erika, who is your dear girlfriend, a Word, begs a motherly Mother Mrs. Runk.

Else fetches the fire wood axe from the cupboard under the sink in the kitchen. Else takes a wide swing with her arm and hacks into the nuptial bed frame. As if wild Else hacks into the beautiful bed stead so that the splinters just fly.

A Mother-in-law Rinx runs up with the noise and splitting.

Stop her, shouts a mother-in-law. The poor thing has gone mad. She will break all the beautiful furniture which is all that we have.

So do stop Else, all three Women prevail on Else with outstretched arms.

Else pecks as if possessed into the wood with the axe. Makes notches with the sheath in the head board. labours like a navvy in a in a wooden mine. The chips split up. The posts crack.

Else!!!

Else does not hear. Else is accomplishing her work today. She has had to wait for it for a long time. Today she is making everything good again. It is only the fault of these stupid pieces of furniture when sometimes everything goes wrong. It is solely the offence of these wrought iron rules that bar every way out. One disposes of them. Done. Do all raise an outcry? Naturally. Cling closely onto it. Onto the mustiness. Onto habit. Onto regulation. Always wanting the whole hand that does not cost anything. Buy themselves into a paradise with indugences. Into a grave site in the sun. Into a future castle in the air that they do not have to build. Else sees through them. A so-called society drives up its so-called Word arsenal and aims all cannons at Else. Else could not care less. A Mother-in-law and a Mother Runk raise an outcry in unison with a so-called friend Erika. They want something. Always want something or the other. Always wanting to take advantage and profit from it.

Else rages in the bedroom. Has to be demolished this abyss of interior decoration. Must be destroyed this subjugating loo vessel. Scratched out this violation zoo. Erika? Erika an accomplice? Erika is able to make Words. No deeds. Crumbles a tip of a knife of rat poison into her Husband's tea once only. Makes a verbose drama out of that. In which Erika plays the main role of course. I hold the pinch and it lights up glows in the light or some such. I mutter a dreadful curse over a cup or some such. A cup of tea or some such. It is supposed to bring you death destruction or something like that! Idle talk. That is all that that Erika is. All that an Erika is looking for is a goal into which her stream of speech discharges. Her verbiage that she cultivates like plants. Something different an Erika does not gather together. Not produce. Mother Runk spices it all with a little glass of home-made eggnog. So that the torrents of Words are a little piquant. So that they fence in those such as stupid speech poor ones like an Else. An Else is stupid enough to believe that Words are somehow minor miracles or something like that. That they can bring this about or something like that. Such an idiot is an Else Rinx! Now she is crammed full of these harpoons like a poor whale catcher full of whales. Else has such a fury for the producers of Words. Wants nothing more than an Else admiration an Else amazement an Else deep vibration to decorate the Wall as a trophy. To cut out a piece for herself from Else with her Words. The best bits of course. Leaves behind a carved up Else in a desert made of intimations and inflexions. Never lets an Else out from her skin sack. Put them together literally into her cells' cell her flesh abbey and shove shut.

Else lunges forward with her axe. One last time. That is it. Now still out with the bulky rubbish into the entrance hall. Like a fury Else scrapes through the door. Scratches up the wall. Scrapes the paint off the door frame. Clatters and crashes so that the people come running. What is the quiet Mrs. Rinx junior doing today! She is such a calm and friendly and quiet woman. She cannot cope with the adversity which affects her. The poor poor Mrs. Rinx. Oh don't take it like that the neighbours soothe. Mother Rinx and Mother Runk together with Erika who is sobbing. You must not take everything so seriously, the neighbours pronounce. Such a case of bereavement can completely unhinge people say the neighbours. In addition such a briefly and happily married Mrs. Rinx, say the neighbours. Something like this passes as quickly as it arises.

The bunch of people stands around the three women who are all weeping now. Unaffected Else moves past them. To and fro. In and out by the door. She flings the patchwork rug into the entrance hall. She rips the antimacassar off the wall and roughly wraps it around the head of Mrs. Rinx. Doesn't the mother-in-law just yelp. Else darts into the room of the Mamma-in-law. There flies a snake skin pump. The other one is held in Else's hand. Cheers, rages Else Rinx the young Widow, cheers to the snake! Cheers to the scum that some pumps bring forth against their will!

Such a poor young widow, who is completely confused, one should give her something to calm her, say the neighbours. They are of course so glad that something is finally happening. They are of course so grateful that a little scandal is in sight. Before their eyes! There the neighbours are not in so much of a hurry with the calming down. A kind Word can already work miracles. One sees that with Mother Runk. And with daughter Erika. They are already looking astonished. Are not crying at all. Otherwise a Mother Runk and a daughter Erika will miss something important in the end. All but all the neighbours stand and wait in anticipation.

Good night, an Else suddenly twitters. Without anyone being able to expect something like that. She closes the flat door shut. Bang. Snap. Bolted.

9. THE INGRATITUDE

It is bright morning. A cheerful light morning. The Mother-in-law Rinx stands at her own flat door. She comes from the Runk family. She had stayed overnight there in a makeshift bed. Her Daughter-in-law Else to wit is not opening the door. So that the Mother-in-law has to declare war from the other side.

Else, rattles Mother-in-law Rinx, Else open up!

Nothing stirs behind the door. A silence prevails over there that is not normal.

Else you will open this door now! drums Mother-in-law Rinx, you will let me in now! Mother Rinx shrills furiously at the threshold. Here a battle is being prepared that will show where a blame is to be found. What then does a Mother-in-law do so that an Else makes so bold! Does not take the Mother-in-law inside.

Else you open this door! a Mother-in-law suddenly rises up, otherwise it will be taken off its hinges. Otherwise who knows what will be exposed. Otherwise all sorts of things will come to light that we as the only Widows Rinx would rather sweep under the patchwork rug. Open up you miserable thing, shouts a Mother-in-law, before everything becomes worse. Annoyance! Worry! Wilfulness!

Just what is it with doors that are always closed to Mrs. Rinx! The Future is closed. The Past is closed in any case. Pleasure is closed. Morality is closed. Which doors is a Mrs. Rinx senior then supposed to dash against? Which coals is she then supposed to carry to anywhere? Mrs. Rinx is quite certainly equipped with a body. Which ages. But does not keep silent. It does not do that by nature. Hunger! it announces. A Mrs. Rinx is hungry. Thirst! it whines shrilly. A Mrs. Rinx is thirsty. Fear Anger Greed! A Mother Rinx wants to cry with anxiety rage desire. A corporeal calling is anchored deeply somewhere in a stature of Mrs. Rinx. Is stuck in a flesh structure like an alphabet in a Word. In person a Mother can be spelled out from a sly deception. A Mother-in-law has not invented that herself. A skin crawls. Shudders through the body, if one touches it. The horror travels through marrow and bones and fallopian tube hollows. The scenery is arranged in a standard series by a nature. A Mrs. Rinx does not take a receptor from off a rack. She does not know at all where a rack is supposed to be. She has never heard anything about it. Such a nature floods a horse-pond of pleasant feeling through a system without question. Ultimately a nature manages the entire works.

Else you stupid cow now clear the entrance! a Mother-in-law hacks figuratively at the door. Either you will now share the home my little castle cupboard with me on the spot, or else. And I am not joking, the Mother Rinx threatens. On the contrary that is a declaration of war. For sure.

A Mother-in-law does not turn a receiver up and down. That is done by a nature alone inside in the body structure. A Mother-in-law does not reach there at all. Even if she wants to. Such a debt collector comes and goes. He stretches himself out in recollection and gives itself airs. Lolls about indecorously in body parts. Heats them up. That is a groaning. Catches a cold from time to time is a wretched same old story in complete secret. A hypothalamus ignites. Wants to reward a Mrs. Rinx! Rich rich lustful recompense! An old Mrs. Rinx. A young Mrs. Rinx. What is the difference already there. It is all the same to a nature. Main thing a nature commands a nature. Switch on. Switch off. Already the nature boy is running as a wild fire across a life relay race. Until it collapses. Old construction. New construction. Flat construction. Superstructure. Hanging garden. Lever horn. It is all the same to a nature.

Else, the Mother-in-law makes a noise at the door-handle. Else! You will be sorry for all this. Everything. Everything! The Mother-in-law shakes and pushes at the gateway to a Justice. She has the right of admission! She is in the right. That is what an instinct tells her. It holds sway in a body. That is a calling. And travels. Travels to and fro on neural paths. Changes. And changes again. And calls and calls! I want a skin! I want flesh! It calls. I am terribly hungry! it calls. And thirsty. And lascivious. As things sometimes come to pass in a Mrs. Rinx! As at an annual fair. Where maypoles are standing. Where brass bands are playing. I am so necessary! A reputation cries for help. I am the nature that requires fresh supplies! New blood! aches the reputation which has something to lose that belongs to nature. The reputation is so right! It needs an echo that looks like a Mrs. Rinx. And it needs an echo that again looks like a miniature version of Mrs. Rinx. And already lurking in that again is an echo that has to get out. And that looks exactly like a Mrs. Rinx. The nature has to reverberate further. Over here with the voracity! Over here with the rind the swallow's tail! Is nobody praising me? Oh yes. Mrs. Rinx loves the strap the beater. She gladly shakes hands with him. Good day. A Mother Rinx takes what a mother nature allows. A nature allows everything. It is namely all the same to her. For what purpose has she given a Widow Rinx a body? To die of starvation? To wither? A Mrs. Rinx does not believe that. A nature is fair. An old Mrs. Rinx. A young Mrs. Rinx. That is really all the same to her. But it is not all the same to an Else. An Else has read too many Mills and Boone-like "Erika" novels. Or? In those an Else is a property offense. Hans is the fenced-off property of Else. This property and these morals are not occupied by anyone else. Only a notary lives as codicil to a contract. A community administration clings to a surplus that a Married Couple produces. A Married Couple is a body corporate and not a body.

Else! Else! a Mother-in-law foams with rage. Now there will be lawful partition! Or do you rather want an awful argument?

Mrs. Rinx senior beats and hammers and scratches at the door. She stabs at the door bell.

The Mother-in-law sits down on the top step of the staircase. It is now all the same to her. What an Else knows will not be believed of a Mother-in-law. A Mrs. Rinx knows pretty much for sure something about the strange death of her son. She will now convey that to a place where they are interested in peculiar ways of dying.

The door opens. An Else is standing there. Pale is an Else and inflamed with rage.

Get lost, Else rudely spits at her Mother-in-law. Push off from here and do not let yourself be seen any more.

Do not say such a thing, says Mrs. Rinx. You will be sorry.

Evaporate into the trouble troposphere or twist into a bush into an umbrella, clanks Else. Into a geranium or tomato.

Do not say such a thing, says Mrs. Rinx. We can still save the situation, Else. You only have to want to.

A Mother-in-law had been stored for long enough in a shoe box apartment. Laid out only for a unique Mr. Rinx, as no real nature envisages. Who unexpectedly drops in and thrashes with the whip. Are the domestic animals well-behaved? Are they docile and willing and cheap? Chop chop!

Drop dead at last you pest! Else bursts out. Melt dissolve you patch of grease! Evaporate you slut! Fade away you useless nuisance you mean old battle axe!

Do not say such a thing, says Mrs. Rinx. Do not speak like that to your Mother-in-law acquired by marriage. Is it not the same whether a copy originates from you or me? Is it not an authenticity into which a fate has sent us?

A Mother-in-law attracts no blame. A body of each Mrs. Rinx writes itself off. Not in business economics. In nature! Also the hogshead of the late departed Mr. Rinx. He writes himself off again and again. Even if imitations are already floating around in superfluity. The copier does not have command of legal writing and the rafts are no salvation on which one does not drown. Nature is just like that. A Mother-in-law Rinx body continues writing itself, just the way it comes along. It is looking for a copy shop where it stands and cheers, too. The transcript becomes completely illegible. If it does not remain only a plan altogether, of no interest to anybody. A design that is not carried out any more. The enthusiasm lacks the gentle voice and the high sky. Does not become a body. Only the hunger returns. The hunger stays.

Else gives the crouching Mother-in-law a shove. A thump. The Mother-in-law almost tips over. She jumps up. Now a Mother-in-law has really had enough. Now a red line has been reached. Has she not tried everything? Has she not continually swallowed almost everything? Did she not tolerate a geranium for as long as she had to! Did she not let herself be put out of action, for as long as she had to!

The door falls gnashing into the jaws of the lock. The wall reverberates a little.

This damage was the last straw. Mrs. Rinx does not permit herself to be maltreated any longer. Violated by all and violating all in return! Mrs. Rinx goes to a police station. Then an Else is gone. Then she straight away gets herself a cat Kitty. Immediately. Then there is calm.

10. AN END

Else is sitting pale on the slat-bed. A long illness is survived. It is a long phase of mildew shimmering away. A rupture a force has broken out from her. A ruin rich with Words is standing around. It was once upon a time an intact house. Once upon a time it was completely new. Once upon a time so beautiful in the decorations and the flourishes. A promise for a long, long time. Until death. Some eras speed so terribly. Demand so diligently incision by incision. No flesh at all, the heavens. So mad-mindedly pale this summer, the nature. Expelled, the colour the noise and the smell. Just tatters. Drift bleached out in the air. Reminds Else of nothing.